Rebel
Tides

Rebel Tides

by Brigit Rosé and Nikki Haras

Published by

Two Realms Publishing LLC

Irmo, SC 29063

https://tworealmspublishingllc.com

Cover Designer: Sweet 15 Designs

Interior Designer: Two Realms Publishing LLC

Editor: Cassandra Fear

Illustrator: Nicodemus Holroyd

Cartographer: Jog Brogzin

Ebook ISBN: 978-1-7346375-9-5

Paperback ISBN (Amazon): 978-1-955106-13-9

Paperback ISBN (Worldwide): 978-1-7346375-1-9

Printed in the United States of America

Content Warning

Welcome to Prisma Isle, a realm not for the faint of heart.

Humans may not exist, but that doesn't mean villages don't have any fucked up shit happening inside their walls. We would warn you of everything, except the list is extensive. And we could be here far longer than necessary. All you need to know is that shit gets bad and escape isn't always possible.

On the brighter side, because let's face it, there has to be one. There's a lot of sex to counteract all that dark.

Except in this book, but we make up for it in the next one.

Yes, we agree.

Balance is the necessity of life.

Dedication

To our fans for your immense patience.

Rebel Tides

PRISMA ISLE™ SERIES

BOOK THREE

BRIGIT ROSÉ & NIKKI HARAS

TWO REALMS PUBLISHING LLC

TERMINOLOGY

Adolescent: term in shape shifter culture for children ten years of age to twenty years of age

Aphros [af-rows]: the second cycle of the Vernal Equinox (the spring)

Antekilio [ant-E-keel-oh]: library of the Sirens

Chicane Village: village of the guilers

Chimera: a lion-like with a snake-like mane, horns, hind legs of a ram, front paws of a bird, a beak-like jaw, and large feather wings

Cycle: approximately one month or from one full moon to the next

Demeter [dee-MEE-ter]: the goddess of fertility, earth, and harvests; protector of marriage and social order; daughter of Cronos and Rhea; mother to Persephone; and creator of the sirens

Full-fledged: term in shape shifter culture for adults; those twenty years of age and older

Galenus [gah-LEE-nus]: male, canine shape shifter, deceased

Guiler [guy-lure]: a humanoid species with elemental abilities

Hades: the Greek god of the underworld; sometimes used as a sort-of curse word by the shape shifters

Informant: soldier to the shape shifter king, Markham

Julunna [jew-lew-na]: the first cycle of the Luminos Equinox (the summer)

Kriah [KREE-uh]: a female nymph who lives in Migas Village

Lacuna [la-KEW-na]: an hour of time

Luminos Equinox [lum-OH-nose]: summer

Manticore: a lion-like creature with a scorpion tail and dragon or bat-like wings

Marana: the second cycle (month) of the year

Métamorphe [met-a-mor-fey]: the shape shifter village

Migas Village [MEE-gahs]: the hidden hybrid village and a place of sanctuary

Mindlink: a telepathic connection between twins and some mates

Nestling: term in the shape shifter culture for children one year of age to five years of age

Newling: term in the shape shifter culture for newborns to one year of age

Penumbra(s) [pah-num-BRAH]: week(s)

Pteryina [ter-EEN-uh]: home of the sirens; adjacent to The Clouds

Saint Beast: the largest of the dragons, possessing the greatest raw physical strength and magical power. Unlike typical sky dragons, they have several rings of fangs

Safe Juice: water

Seiphinx [SEF-InKS]: a creature with the head and front torso of a bird (sparrow), back torso and tail of a lion, and gold beak; they are battle-intense creatures created for the warriors of Migas Village

Seplugh: the third cycle of the Luminos Equinox (the summer)

Siren: these bird-like creatures were created by Demeter. From the thighs up, they have the body of a human female/male; from the thighs down, their legs narrow into those of a sparrow with talons for feet

Solaris: year, which comprises sixteen cycles (months) for the inhabitants of Prisma Isle

Umbra(s) [um-BRAH]: day(s)

Vasilia [vuh-SILL-ee-uh]: female siren that is the Elder of the sirens and lives in Pteryrina

Verdant Grove: home of the fae

Vernal Equinox [ver-NAL]: spring

Youngling: term in shape shifter culture for children five years of age to ten years of age

Zancle's Rock [Zan-kuls rock]: bar and restaurant in the marketplace run by Ambrosia; known for their venison stew

Chapter One

Thalasia glanced over her shoulder at the humanoid-creature. It resembled a human, except for the magic it seemed to possess and the pint-sized, bony wings protruding from its back. At least it couldn't fly with those things. She turned and ran out of the forest toward the beach. None of this had been what she'd searched for since her arrival.

All she had to find—stepping out of the edge of the forest, her eyes fell upon a bridge about fifty feet in front of her. *Finally!* The bridge from her vision swarmed ahead. Now, she just had to—a swoosh of air came up behind her, lifted her in the air, and slammed her backside down on the ground.

Fuck! Her left wing burned as grains of sand made their way into the gaping hole in her appendage. Thalasia pushed up on her hands and spotted the humanoid-creature fast approaching. She got on her feet. He could manipulate the air. Well, she could too.

In more ways than one.

Tired of running, she opened her mouth and sang. Her angelic voice carried across the wind and soothed the anger the creature compelled. Her song didn't require words, just the melody. As she closed the distance between her and the humanoid, her aria stilled the wild wind and its manipulator.

She placed one hand at the nape of its neck and reached for the dagger tucked into the belt of her pants. With one swift move, she removed the blade from its hiding place and thrust it into the creature's gut.

It grunted as black blood spewed from its wound, and then it dropped to the ground with a thud.

Her heart pounded beneath her chest. The last of the tune left her lips. Thalasia leaned over, yanked her dagger from its body, and wiped it clean using her pants. There was no time to waste.

She didn't know how many of those things had followed her. Returning the dagger to its rightful spot, she took off for the bridge.

Her talons dug into the gritty white grains as she ran toward freedom. It took longer to reach the bridge than if she could've flown. Damn arrow had taken a small chunk out of her wing. It'd be useless for the next day.

With the bridge a few feet away, Thalasia stopped. The first board of the wooden overpass had some sort of weird engraving. Studying the image, she walked closer and looked across it. Well, half the bridge. Fog gathered somewhere around the middle, a good thirty yards ahead. Still, each board had a different engraving, although after so many, they began repeating. One caught her eye.

Five or six panels in—she noticed a familiar lyre.

Her ears prickled. She peered over her shoulder. This was the bridge in her vision. As for what she'd just seen, there was no time to contemplate it.

Thalasia started across the bridge. Half-way across, the fog grabbed her and yanked her through some invisible field. The barrier rippled outward as it carried her forward and tossed her out the other side. Her legs and arms flailed for a moment until she face-planted and landed in more white sand.

With a small groan, she pushed up on her arms and faced the shield that had been there. It billowed out in an iridescent wave.

What the hell?

Her pulse quickened. Where in Good Demeter had she ended up? Another realm? Getting to her feet, Thalasia scanned her surroundings. A tall cliff stood a few feet away. Behind her, the waves crashed into one another as the sun set below the horizon.

Nothing about this flight—her mind's eye opened and tossed her against the jagged rock of the towering cliff-side.

In her head, the scenery changed. The beachy sand disappeared and, in its stead, she saw overgrown grass and a forest full of thick, tall trees. The surrounding woods were so lush she almost missed the dark-haired person with green wings that ran by. Not that she noticed the face. Or the eyes. But something about this person... it seemed familiar.

Thalasia gasped as the vision left her head and practically threw her back to the pebbly sands beneath her feet. She leaned against the rugged seaside cliff and closed her eyes to settle her thundering heartbeat.

Man, things really needed to get easier.

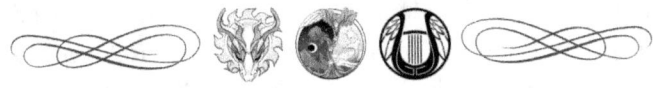

Winding her way through the clouds, Aurelia easily spotted the source of the disturbance. A substantial tear shimmered an iridescent rainbow over the beach, near the foot of the Stairway to Heaven—the bridge that once permitted the earthbound species to rise above the clouds to visit the draconic cities. She watched intently as a strange creature exited the gateway. Her vision zeroed in on the blue-feathered woman as she dug her talons into the white sands.

A nasty snarl curled her lips, exposing her fangs. She rushed to the beach, her amethyst scales shedding in a flurry of gold particles and white sand. Only a few of her draconic features remained—her menacing reptilian eyes rimmed by dark purple scales with a powerful glow and her fearsome fangs. Just enough to strike fear into this exotic newcomer.

"What have you done?" Aurelia demanded.

The girl's distant, glossed over stare cooled the dragoness's rage, depriving it of its potency as she watched the other woman collapse. She caught her by the arm, careful not to dig her gilded nails into the female's flesh, and she held the woman steady until she found her balance. Whoever she was, this girl was cursed with a terrible affliction.

She possessed the sight.

"Easy. I've got you," Aurelia murmured. The remnants of her rage dissipated, releasing on the tails of her power as she reverted to her human form. No eyes, no scales. Just flesh and bone.

Aurelia's gaze drifted to the girl's wounded wing. She clasped two of the metal talons in her teeth, her fingertips emitting a warm, golden energy that brushed the wound, smearing it with enriched stardust.

The dazed bird-girl recoiled, a hiss escaping her lips as she returned to herself. Aurelia's magic must have brought her back to reality from... wherever her far-off stare had taken her.

Wincing, the girl attempted to pull away. "What're you doing?"

"Tending your wound," Aurelia said around the jewelry clamped between her fangs as she maneuvered the appendage gently, inspecting for further damage and mobility as the medicine did its job.

Once, she allowed the female to back away while she replaced her talons on the appropriate fingers. "What did you see?" Aurelia pressed. "Better yet, what attacked you?" She scanned the beach but found no signs of the attacker, only a few drops of the woman's blood staining the sand a brilliant scarlet. Her opponent, or opponents, must still be on the other side.

Crossing her arms, the bird-girl narrowed her silver eyes and sneered. "Doesn't matter. It's dead."

Aurelia's rage threatened to reignite at the other woman's nonchalant response. "Oh, it matters," she growled through clenched teeth, forcing herself to take a deep breath before continuing. "If it has friends, they might come through. That pathway"—She gestured toward the open bridge—"isn't closing. There has to be a reason." She fought to keep her emotions in check as the full weight of the situation settled. Nothing like this had ever happened before—not to her knowledge. Once she resolved this situation with the bird-girl, she'd need to consult Seru—and his library.

"Seeing as I've never been here before, I couldn't tell you." The girls smirked and started down the beach, her talons kicking up tiny grains of sand with each step.

The bird-girl paused and glanced over her shoulder. "I can tell you it's one of those things on Candescent Isle. At least, I believe that's what they called it."

"Never heard of it." For all she knew, the girl had made up the names and places. Aurelia used her magic to reappear in the woman's path, forcing her to an abrupt halt. "If you think you're going to walk or fly away, you're wrong. The longer that gate remains open, the more unstable the magic in this realm becomes. And when that happens, even your fortunes aren't going to save you."

Frowning, the girl rolled her eyes. "I'm assuming you live here, or at least near here. Seeing as it would cause some issues, don't you think it would be prudent to figure out how to close it? And sweetheart, if you don't have the answers, then I'm sure there's someone here who does."

Aurelia wrinkled her nose at the suggestion. "Only earthbound live on the ground, bird. The only reason I'm here is to ensure your disturbance doesn't lead to more trouble." So, the woman didn't know how to close the portal... did that mean she wasn't the one who opened it? Aurelia's brows knitted together, still refusing to yield to the stranger.

As her internal questions led to more questions, Aurelia's frustration mounted. *Someone who does...* A thought occurred to her. "Enoch!"

In an instant, Aurelia shifted and took to the skies.

Rising to her feet, Thalasia partially extended her left wing but didn't get more than a quarter of its full length. She grimaced at the spot where she'd lost a few feathers. Stupid creature had caught her with an arrow and knocked her to the ground.

The cave seemed massive. She could easily see an extensive tunnel beyond her current location. Big enough to live in. It wouldn't be ideal, but after her interaction with the dragon-shifter a few hours ago, it was better than the alternative.

Aside from the crackling fire, the moon provided the only other light in the cave. Thalasia squeezed the muscle in her shoulder one last time and glanced back out at the night sky. Her gaze fell to the bridge she'd spent hours watching. Yes, she'd left the creature's remains on the other side, so at some point someone would discover it. That didn't mean the broken barrier was her fault. How could it be?

Maybe she wasn't like every other siren, but she didn't possess the power to break a barrier. At least she didn't think so. Even if she wasn't normal by siren standards, this couldn't be her fault. No matter what the dragon-girl had insinuated, no one could blame her.

This wasn't the time to fret over something so coincidental. Thalasia stretched out on her makeshift nest of sticks and moss. It would suffice for the night. She had to rest for her wing to heal. By morning, it would be restored, and then she'd be ready to continue her search.

Something landed with a thud at her feet, startling her from the slumber she hadn't begun. Metal against stone soon followed.

Thalasia cracked open an eye and shifted her gaze toward the noise. A human-looking creature with spiky black hair, dark eyes, black-rimmed glasses, and shackles half-stood at the end of her bed.

The dragoness returned with a small gilded army at her back, their golden armor reflecting the flames of the dwindling campfire. Another group emerged from the darkened tunnel, each boasting the finest weapons she'd ever seen. They'd cut off every exit.

"I'll have whatever *catalyst* you used to open the barrier, blue bird." It was no longer a request, but a demand. The dragon-shifter held out a taloned hand, expecting full compliance.

What in Demeter's name? Thalasia jerked upright. She crossed her arms and frowned. *Catalyst?* "What part of 'I didn't open the damn thing' didn't you comprehend? Are you just that stupid? Or was that information too much for your brain to handle?"

"According to the expert here"—The dragon-girl nodded to the nearby creature, who still scrambled in the dirt, his lips to the ground as if he was grateful to be alive—"you're lying. Enoch! Quit your groveling and get on with it," the girl reprimanded, delivering a swift kick to his backside.

He stumbled forth, nearly landing in Thalasia's lap. "P-pardon me, young lady ..." He offered a forced smile. It didn't take long for his black eyes to be drawn to the chain adorning her neck and glistening in the firelight. "The matriarch requests to borrow your—" he gestured toward the golden necklace.

Good Demeter, of all the creatures to run into, she had to find the darkest of them. Her silver eyes lit up the cavern as she narrowed her gaze at the dragon-girl. Gods, dragon-shifters really had a way about them. Thalasia stood and offered a hand to the human-like creature at her feet, then refocused her attention on the so-called matriarch. Bitch was more like it. "I don't give a shit who the hell you think you are. No one deserves to be treated like dirt."

The dragon-shifter's lips tugged into a toothy sneer. She chuckled. "He might appear harmless to you now, but Enoch is no saint, I assure you. He could live a thousand lifetimes and never escape the weight of his sins. Remove those shackles and see how your kindness serves you, siren."

"It might surprise you how far kindness will get you. I don't know you. Nor have you bothered to try asking for anything. While I appreciate the aid you gave my wing, it'll heal on its own." Thalasia snorted. "I don't tolerate bullies, and obviously you've got some kind of stick up your ass."

She crossed her arms again and drank in the full sight of the army dragon-girl brought along with her. "Case in point, you seem to think me, a single siren, is pretty dangerous. Instead of trying to ask for my help, you brought an army along. How far do you think that'll get you?"

Enoch winced at her biting remark. "Never wise to piss off the queen," he whispered, leaning in as he offered the advice.

Dragon-girl inclined her chin, meeting Thalasia's silvery glare with her violet one. "Anyone who recklessly jumps through realms are dangerous. I won't allow you, your flock, or any other to bring your troubles to my door. Funny, I don't recall you knocking or requesting passage through our lands last we spoke, either. You stormed off, leaving your problems to be dealt with by others. As you're within my lands, that responsibility falls to me and my people. I assure you, there's no trouble in being prepared when dealing with someone as charming as you," the dragon-shifter proclaimed.

Thalasia raised an eyebrow. Her flock? Had she landed somewhere near the home of the sirens? A place she'd never set foot in before. This was news to her. Then again, she didn't exactly know where she'd ended up to begin with. Her lips curled into a small smile. "One: I don't know what flock you're talking about. Two: I didn't storm off, I walked away... from you. I've spent the last few hours watching the bridge. Three: I didn't recklessly jump. The fog grabbed me and tossed me here. It didn't exactly give me a choice. Now, if you want to figure out what happened, I'd be happy to talk to your so-called expert." She shifted her gaze toward Enoch, who still hovered nearby. "Without your army. Unless you're incapable of acting like an adult."

"If you've been watching, then I'm sure by now you've realized the situation isn't going anywhere." The dragon-girl's violet eyes twinkled for a moment. She let out a heated breath and turned to the men behind her. "Half of you wait outside; the rest go guard the bridge." The dragon-shifter proceeded to those across from her. "You lot, retreat to the end of the tunnel and no further."

The towering men and women shuffled uneasily.

"I said OUT!" the dragon-shifter roared, stirring them into action.

Enoch nearly jumped out of his skin before retreating closer to the siren.

As the last of the elite guard filed out, the dragon-shifter focused on Thalasia. "Make no mistake, if you try anything, I'm more than capable of subduing you myself. As I'm sure your new *friend* here will tell you."

Enoch took the moment's silence to steal a glance at Thalasia, never quite allowing the necklace she wore out of his sight.

Reaching up, Thalasia stroked the back of Enoch's head, much like a mother comforting her child. She didn't know them, but the situation had to be de-escalated, and he was staring at her just a little too much. Specifically, the gold chain around her neck. The trinket itself remained hidden beneath her tank top. It held no power that anyone should sense, so it made no sense why his attention was so focused on it. No matter, it belonged to her mother, and she would protect it at all costs. "I'm aware that it isn't closing the way it should. How long has the barrier been in place?"

Enoch relaxed into her tender touch. He cleared his throat before replying, his voice low and raspy. "Mm... about three-hundred years, give or take."

Dragon-girl's violet eyes flicked from him to Thalasia.

He swallowed and then proceeded. "The barrier was erected after the Great War, when the species diverged and the last of the witches perished. Both sirens and dragons came here, taking to the skies, while others remained on the ground. An interspecies war broke out among the sirens about a hundred years after the Great War. Shortly afterward, the barrier appeared."

Thalasia blinked. Continuing to stroke Enoch's head, her gaze shifted past the dragon-girl toward the bridge. She had seen multiple engravings on the panels. Looking back at Enoch, she raised an eyebrow. "Do you know who built the barrier? Or how they did it?"

Enoch tilted his head. "There are many theories. The most common states it was erected to keep something out. To preserve the utopia herein."

The dragon-shifter snorted.

"The dragons despised the guilers, grew weary of their abuse of magic and... experimentation." Enoch's words dripped with sourness. "The silver queen... the previous matriarch."

He sat up, reached into the remnants of the fire, and retrieved a stick with which to sketch out his scene, the wooden point scratching out the epic battle in the ashes. "She's said to be the one who put an end to the last enchantress, burning her—and her bird—alive for their treachery..."

Catching a slight change in his demeanor as his story abruptly ended, Thalasia's stance stiffened, so she didn't roll her eyes. Good Demeter, this matriarch needed a serious attitude adjustment. Replaying Enoch's story in her mind, she glanced over her shoulder at the night sky and turned back to him. It certainly explained a few things. "I'm going to assume the theories remain unproven. If we don't know what caused the barrier in the first place, then we have no way of knowing what would've broken it. That said, the best way to figure out what happened is to find out how and who built it. Wouldn't you agree?"

To that matter, it also seemed she now had a name for the creature she'd killed earlier. "And that thing I fought on the other side; would it be safe to presume that's a guiler?"

Enoch pushed his thick-rimmed glasses up his nose with a nod, black smudges appearing where his fingers touched. "Most barriers require a catalyst, or a key to be opened and closed." He briefly glanced at the dragon-shifter before allowing his eyes to drift back to Thalasia's necklace. "When the matriarch appeared demanding answers, naturally I thought you were the only possibility. But it appears she may have... jumped to a few hasty conclusions before gathering all the facts."

He shifted uncomfortably, like an animal awaiting another lashing. When it didn't come, he continued. "Either you, lovely siren, or that fallen guiler must possess an item that allowed the barrier to reopen. Did you see anything of that sort? It needn't be remarkable or extraordinary. Perhaps you noticed the guiler enacting a chant, spell, or magic which may have led to the bridge?"

His words made perfect sense to her. Everything she'd learned about magical barriers indicated the item could be small or even insignificant. Thalasia frowned. "I can't say I noticed anything with the guiler, but he had magic. Air magic. Every one of them I saw on Candescent Isle had magic. I thought it was strange because I've seen no human with magic, not that they were entirely human either." That wasn't entirely true, but they didn't look like witches or warlocks. And she certainly refused to share more than was necessary with these folks.

Otherwise, they could cause further unwanted problems.

Chapter Two

Aurelia sighed, her mind wandering while the deranged scientist and siren took turns exchanging information and questions. Watching him cozy up to the bird-girl made her stomach churn. That she showered him with tender affection, oblivious to his intent to use her to escape when the time came, rose bile in the back of her throat. She did her best to ignore them.

As the siren was the only one to come through, it stood to reason she had the key. Whether she was safeguarding it or simply too daft to realize she had it on her, Aurelia didn't know. But she had no intention of letting the siren out of her sight soon. Nor did she intend to leave Enoch alone and unsupervised with their strange new friend. Lest he craftily persuade his way out of his bindings and decide to cross realms, promptly closing and sealing the barrier once on the other side. Instead, she focused on the bridge.

"What do you mean 'not entirely human?'" Enoch probed.

"They look like deformed humans," the siren said.

"Curious..." Enoch sounded truly fascinated. "Perhaps we should inspect, my queen? See what these strange new evolved guilers are for ourselves."

Aurelia stood, dusting off her satin gown. "Yes, *we*. Not you." She gestured to one guard, who took hold of Enoch's arm and hoisted him to his feet. The scientist gave an exaggerated whimper, slumping in the much–larger man's grasp. "Come, siren. Let's investigate this guiler of yours."

The siren glanced from the guard, Enoch, and Aurelia and shook her head. Shifting her eyes back to her wings, she extended them out completely, a full ten feet across the cave. Her silver eyes lit the cavern as a small smile tugged at the corners of her lips. "You know, dragon, it wouldn't kill you to say please. You may not fully trust me or Enoch over here, but he seems full of information. Though I have one question before we jump on this train. Do you know what other species live... wherever this is?"

"Prisma Isle," Enoch informed, sulking as he stayed true to his nature. He crumpled to the ground, forcing the guard to carry his full weight.

Aurelia rolled her eyes at his theatrics. "The continent is Prisma Isle. The Land of Clouds is home to the dragons," she amended, pointing to the sky beyond the confines of the cave. "Drakes cast out by my predecessor roam the lands. Tiny beasts stripped of most of their power for defecting during the war and siding with the guilers, among others. Manticores and others exist to the north, amid the forests near to Mysteria Mountains. The chimera reside in the southern region. Shape shifters keep to a small village within the forest. Plus, varying species live in the enchanted forest and beyond. And, last but not least, the sirens stay in the skies out of draconic reach in a region known as Pteryrina."

The young siren raised an eyebrow at Enoch, then she turned her full attention to Aurelia and nodded. "Well, that certainly explains a lot. Shall we?"

Bearing a grin, she didn't wait for Aurelia to agree. The siren took off for the cave's mouth, her talons scraping against the stone. With a quick leap from the opening and a brief flap of her wings, she soared through the night sky toward the bridge.

Her golden hair whipped in the currents swirling inside the cave. Aurelia allowed the wild winds generated by the siren's flashy takeoff to settle.

"Bring him," she growled. "I may yet require his 'wealth of knowledge.'" She cloud-stepped her way to the bridge, leaving the others to catch up.

Aurelia found her regent bowing an introduction to the siren, low and elegant, as if she belonged among the best of them. He paid her too high an honor, one she didn't yet deserve.

The siren smiled. "Seru, it's wonderful to meet you. I'm Thalasia."

He seemed to catch Aurelia's glare and straightened in response, smoothly switching gears to attend her with a quick rundown of his observations.

Cocking her head, Thalasia peered over her shoulder at Aurelia, her multi-colored blue wings tucked in tight. "Nice of you to join us." With a smirk, she focused on Seru and walked forward, gesturing to the boards. "I'm sure you've noticed the symbols engraved on the panels across the bridge. To me, it says this bridge and its barrier are linked to this land: Prisma Isles. While it would be easy to blame me, you can't ignore the fact that there is a possibility there is something going on in the land. You may know the species, but have you had any contact with them to discern if there have been any changes to their parts of the continent?"

Seru stepped between Aurelia and the siren. "Thalasia may be correct, Regina. The engravings alternate, repeating in pattern and color." He indicated each board on the rainbow bridge with his quill. "If I had to hazard a guess, I'd say they're emblems—one for each species present on the continent. The ambassadors permitted to grace the Land of Clouds have seemed... uneasy in recent years. I've heard mention of many disturbances—infertility, illness, loss of crops. The imbalances could indicate a shift in the magics that govern all the lands."

"Uneasy? In what way?" Enoch piped up from where the guard held him at bay, a safe distance from the bridge. He peeked around a wall of polished gold. "Oh, hello there, Seru. I almost didn't recognize you. Looks as though you've risen since last I saw you, no longer doing the queen's dirty work, eh? What a pity. Rending the land red with the blood of innocents suited you." He couldn't keep the grin from his face until a harsh static rippled through the clearing. A snap of electricity pierced the scientist, momentarily silencing him.

Thalasia's nose wrinkled. Grimacing, she stroked her throat and rolled her shoulders. Her face consumed by disgust, she muttered, "Fucking destiny." Shaking her head, she shifted her glower from Enoch and softened her gaze as she looked at Seru and Aurelia. "In order to understand everything, we need to visit the other species."

"So, it would seem," Seru confirmed, dipping his chin and exposing the red tint coloring his cheeks. After a moment, the regent returned his attention to their task. "In order to proceed, we must learn of the plights of the earthbound and reacquaint ourselves with the land. We can join forces with Thalasia until we have resolved these matters."

Aurelia's displeasure washed over them in a scalding heat, her lips recoiling to expose her fangs.

Crossing her arms, Thalasia half-covered a stifled yawn. Her eyes drifted to her fingers, to the white grains of sand, and finally landed on Aurelia. "That's okay. I'm happy to do it alone."

"Oh, spare us your lone ranger bull." Aurelia turned on her. "You'd be lost before your eyes rose above the cliff-side."

She stole a moment to collect her thoughts before proceeding. "Seru and I will go with the siren. Jaeriko will escort our unruly prisoner back to his cell. Vera"—Aurelia shoved down her pride before naming her suitor—"and Cynric will take my seat in court until we return."

"Regina—"

"You may return to collect anything we might need for our journey. I think the Cloud Court and the Sky Temple can behave themselves while we uncover the source and cause of these disturbances."

Seru bowed his head in compliance. "May I fetch you anything, Thalasia? I'm afraid I'm not as well versed in your species' needs as I am in our own."

"Not yours. Just hers." Enoch's raspy voice, rougher than usual, came as he hauled himself upright. The guard took hold of him and ferried him back to his fortress in the low-hanging clouds before another fight could ensue.

Interlacing her fingers, Thalasia offered a small dip of her chin to Seru. "Thank you. I appreciate the offer, but I found food along the forest's edge before making a nest in the cave." Tensing her shoulders, she narrowed her silver eyes at Aurelia. "If I were you, I'd stop assuming I'm useless. I guarantee I've seen more in my life than the time you've been in that high and almighty chair you believe has given you the right to behave like a petulant child. As a word of advice, it would be best if you lost the attitude before we speak to any of the other species around here. Otherwise, we'll get nowhere fast. Think you can handle that?"

Aurelia opened her mouth, ready to break what few restraints remained intact after an evening in such trying company, but Seru interceded on her behalf once more, saving them all the headache and destruction.

"I don't believe that will be a problem," Seru said. "Most earthbound fear or worship dragons—we're akin to gods. Not unlike your Demeter. Though, as a precaution, I think it best we lie low and try not to draw too much unwanted attention to ourselves until we've achieved a better grasp of the situation, and better gauged the temperament of our company. Now, if you ladies will excuse me." Seru disappeared into the night.

"Hmm ..." Thalasia's gaze leveled on Aurelia. "Have a good night, Your Highness." The last two words dripped with sarcasm. Saying nothing else, she shot into the sky and flew off.

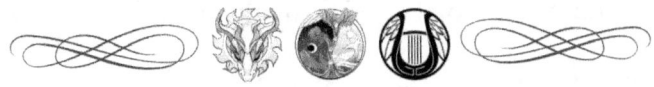

No species she'd ever dealt with had been this difficult before. Yes, she'd always had to observe them. It came with the territory. Not that these dragon-shifters—and whatever Enoch was—appeared any different. The so-called matriarch had already noticed the one thing she worked so hard to keep hidden. Although it seemed she had successfully redirected the female's attention elsewhere. But it wasn't the only secret she had to protect.

Thalasia stared out from her perch in the highest tree along the forest edge. No way she could return to the cave, not after their discovering her there earlier. She'd sat on these branches for a good hour. It was necessary to ensure that no one followed her before she took action.

None of those she'd met could be trusted.

Certain she was alone, Thalasia removed the lyre charm from beneath her tank top. What the hell? She lifted the trinket and eyed its strings. Two had snapped off. Shit. When had that happened?

Lifting her gaze back out to the deep blue sky, she swung her eyes toward the bridge. She could make out the dragon-shifter's form. The young woman had likely stayed to study the bridge.

Her entrance to Prisma Isle. That had to be when the strings on the lyre broke, rendering it useless. The fog had tossed her into this realm, which had been followed by... *damn it*. It could've occurred when her vision had thrown her up against the cliff side.

Sighing, Thalasia shook her head. It didn't change what she had to do. She reached for the blade tucked in the back of her waistband and partially extended her left wing. It had fully healed, minus a few feathers that had yet to reform. It served as the perfect hiding place.

She sliced open her skin without feathers. Grimacing at the pain, Thalasia inhaled a deep breath and continued to cut out a small pocket in her wing. For all of Demeter, it hurt like hell, but it had to be done. Enoch and the Matriarch had spent too much time with their eyes on the chain around her neck.

Her mother's words replayed in her mind as she clutched the charm in her fist. *Keep it hidden. Let no one see it. It's as special as you are.* She scrubbed her face and tucked the tiny golden lyre into the pocket she'd created. A burning sensation lanced through her body as the two-inch cut healed.

Exhaling, Thalasia looked out over the night sky once again and returned the blade to its hiding spot. Would they notice the lack of weight on the chain? She couldn't take the chance they would. Although Seru hadn't seemed to pay it any mind, she was positive it would come up between him and the matriarch—a woman whose name she still didn't know. It hadn't been hard to notice the way he placated the bitchy queen.

She wasn't the first stick-in-the-mud-almighty-pain-in-the-ass she'd had to deal with. Thalasia suspected she wouldn't be the last, either. With a small snicker, she broke off a piece of bark and collected some moss. She formed it into the outer shape of a lyre, attached it to the golden chain, and tucked it back inside her tank top. It wasn't the best option, but it would do.

For now.

Readjusting in her new nest, she scrutinized the bridge. Could Enoch and the dragon-shifter have been right? Could the broken barrier be her fault? Did she truly possess the key? No. It couldn't be possible. The lyre wasn't meant for that. Neither of her parents had ever mentioned anything about a barrier. Or the lyre as a key. Of any kind.

But maybe... what if they'd done it to protect her? Maybe the journal could tell her something. Except she'd read it from front to back. If it had, she would've remembered. Thalasia pinched the bridge of her nose. There was almost no way around it. She'd have to go to Pteryrina and find some answers.

Without giving up the charm or revealing the truth to anyone. Least of all that female dragon-shifter.

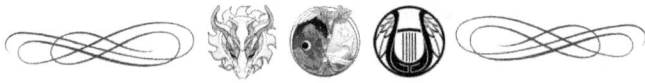

Aurelia said nothing, ever watchful of the rainbow bridge. As her eyes fell to the strange harp gracing the blue board, her hand slipped into the folds of her dress and she held up the glowing crystal she'd confiscated from Enoch. The living core of a star was the purest source of magic in existence. And there were dozens scattered over the isle, raw and waiting to fall into the wrong hands. She needed to locate and secure them before that happened.

In the meantime, this tiny crystal would be more than enough of a boost to deal with whatever came their way. As the others departed, Aurelia finally allowed the rage she'd worked hard to contain unfurl. It blossomed into a roaring flame in her palm, growing until its pink, blue, and purple tongues lashed out, illuminating the white sands in an array of color.

Screaming her frustrations to the winds, Aurelia hurled the celestial flame across the bridge, where it slammed into the cliffs. An enormous crater, scorched black by the flame's intensity, marred the glowing embers of the limestone.

She pressed her taloned thumb and forefinger into her eyes. It did little to dull the wave of exhaustion or quell the rising sense of dread. If they didn't sort this out soon, it could spell disaster. She wandered off, dragging her feet through the sands until she came to a sole driftwood log, its surface worn smooth from its days at sea. She resigned herself to staring at the bridge, memorizing the alternating color pattern and distinct symbols etched in each.

"Vera sends her regards." Seru handed off a knapsack to Aurelia, where she sat atop a driftwood log.

"Thanks," she muttered, weighing the bag in her hand. "Light as a feather." She cringed inwardly at the observation. That silly siren was swiftly becoming more of a headache than she was worth. Aurelia imagined her cooking up some clever scheme in the brush while she stood watch over the bridge.

"Crafted with magic that compresses space," Seru offered, taking a seat next to her. "I've never seen you so downtrodden with the promise of an adventure so close to your fingertips. You've even escaped selecting your first tribute. What troubles you?"

She gave him a strained smile. She appreciated his concern, but as always, he saw through the façade. "Looks like you'll have to take his place," she teased, her voice sounding deflated and tired, even to her. "As the sole male on this venture, it would seem you get the pleasure of that blue-feathered chicken and your new matriarch. You've got to be the unluckiest man on this forsaken island."

Seru managed a bitter chuckle. "Oh, I don't know about that... I'd be honored to even be considered an option among such a pair of fiery and spirited young women."

"Even the bird?" Aurelia gave the face the comment deserved.

"Yes, Majesty, even Thalasia has value." He paused. "You two aren't that different. You're both powerful forces of nature. You should try to smooth the feathers that have been ruffled. She's much more valuable as an ally than an enemy."

She dug her toes into the soft sands, frowning. Her talons bit in the porous wood.

"You may even surprise yourself and make a friend," he suggested when no response came.

Aurelia snorted, unable to keep the laughter out of her tone. "You've got to be joking. Dragons eat birds, Seru. We don't befriend them. There's a reason the sirens stay in Pteryrina."

"Perhaps, as the stars have shown, it's time for all that to change."

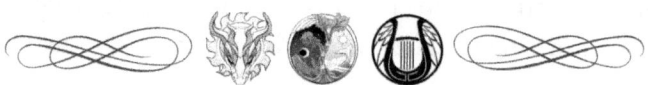

Thalasia flew overhead, enjoying a moment in the morning sky with the sun beating down on her back before landing on the shore. She had a good night's rest with no further interruptions from the dragons. Her wing had fully healed, new feathers and all. The hues of the new feathers were a darker blue than across the rest of her wing. She nodded first to Seru, then to the dragon-shifter pain-in-her-ass. Why had she agreed to this journey with these two again? Right, answers. Ones she hoped to get without difficulty. "Good morning."

"Good morning, Thalasia," Seru replied, smiling warmly.

Dragon-girl stayed in her place on the driftwood log, likely as she had all night.

"Regina, we—"

"Morning..." the dragon-girl mumbled, slinging a bag over her shoulder as she rose. "Let's get a move on before sleeping beauty's coma for a few fancy new feathers lands us at the end of days."

"Forgive her, Thalasia," Seru apologized. "She's not one to remain idle in the face of a good puzzle, or in this case, a problem."

No shit. Thalasia smirked. Wait, that's right... she'd forgotten that dragons required less rest. She rolled her eyes and crossed her arms. "I didn't rest for some new feathers, dragon-girl. I rested because I've been on the move for the last two weeks. Plus, sometimes a good puzzle is better solved in the daylight."

With a shake of her head, she looked between Seru and the dragon-shifter. "Anyone bother to see if the guiler I killed is still over there?"

Dragon-girl scowled.

"I thought we might take your lead in that matter..." Seru started, reaching out to rest a hand on the dragon-girl's arm. She promptly came to a halt in front of the bridge. "I think it best if Thalasia and I cross first, in the event the barrier is unstable or we somehow trigger it to re-close."

The dragon-shifter planted her feet in the sand, ready to argue.

"If there are more of these guilers, you're the best chance we have at deterring an invasion. The guards will follow your command." Seru placed a hand on his chest. "The Land of Clouds—all of Prisma Isle—requires your protection. I'm but a mere advisor. If I were to be trapped, or worse, there'd be little loss."

Dragon-girl nodded her consent before narrowing her eyes, which were brimming with power, in Thalasia's direction. "If anything happens, I'm holding you responsible. So, don't even bother returning without him."

Thalasia stood there, listening to the two of them. Although Seru probably placated himself to her royal highness more than needed, he cared for the woman. Something she hadn't had in nearly eight years. She frowned, scrubbing the memory before it reached her eyes. Tilting her head, she cocked an eyebrow at the girl. "Leave Seru? That wouldn't happen. I like him."

Shifting her gaze to the man of the hour, she dipped her chin at the bridge. "Shall we?"

Seru followed her lead, nervously slipping a finger inside the metal band encircling his neck. He stepped onto the bridge, hesitating a moment. When nothing bad came calling, he trailed behind the pair of blue wings, heaving a sigh of relief.

Glancing over her shoulder, Thalasia noted the moment of hesitation and slowed her pace until they were both certain he'd be fine going across. If she was lucky, the creature's body would be right where she'd left it and they could investigate unscathed. Not because she wouldn't protect Seru, because she would. She just didn't need her secret bubbling back to the surface. Looking back at the collar around Seru's neck, she nodded at it. "Mind if I ask what that thing is?"

He reacted like a child caught stealing a forbidden sweet as his gaze met hers from beneath his thick black lashes. "Ah, you may." Seru swallowed, dropping his hand to his side as they crossed. "It's a gift from the previous Matriarch, the woman who created me. An... instrument to ascertain her influence and will. It links me to her, ensuring I don't stray from the path she intended. I suppose you could say it controls my fate."

Thalasia jerked back as her silver eyes widened a bit. She didn't expect him to answer. Nor did she expect the answer he gave. It almost seemed ironic to share anything with either Seru or his leader. Thalasia's features softened as her eyebrows drew together. She understood him all too well. "We should all be allowed to choose our own path. Too bad destiny, or fate, as you called it, doesn't work like that."

"Reality is a cruel mistress, indeed. There's no shame in resisting her unkind rule," Seru agreed. "Though that's not to say there won't be a hefty penalty in doing so. Those risks, those choices, make us different from those who seek to control us. I used to believe the deeds I committed in Her name simply to save my hide were unforgivable. However, in time—and with the kindness and support of a certain fierce purple princess—I discovered even I had some say in the way my destiny played out."

"Not everyone has that luxury." The goddess ensured that didn't happen to her. It didn't mean she hadn't tried, because she'd battled her visions for almost a year after she'd found herself all alone in the world. At least until her view changed.

Thalasia stopped as they stepped off the bridge. She surveyed the area. Her gaze stopped momentarily on a charred spot along the cliff. When had that happened? She shook the question off. The guiler's body should've been about fifty feet away, right at the edge of the forest, but it wasn't. The two guilers waiting just beyond the trees caught her attention. She hissed at Seru. "Go back!"

The bridge creaked underfoot as Seru tensed at Thalasia's call. Across the clearing, two oddly contorted figures stood within the cover of the trees. One resembled a golem with a tough, stony exterior, and his friend, though alive and well, seemed to match Thalasia's earlier description—a skeletal creature.

To cover their retreat, Seru opened some internal lid enough to allow a blanket of white-hot electrical energy to flow forth, spilling outward around Thalasia and over the land before rising to create a temporary barrier between them and the two creatures lurking in wait. The energy crackled and snapped.

The collar responded to Seru's power, coming alive with a searing heat as it constricted around his throat.

Well, shit. That was pretty impressive. Not her plan, but impressive. Thalasia reached for the steel blade in her waistband. It might be better to attack with her power rather than her knife. Less likely a vision would occur unless—

The two guilers separated, each coming out of the forest in opposite directions.

Of course not, no chance of that happening. One of them looked similar to the one she'd fought yesterday. Great... more air manipulation. That she could handle, except... shit, she didn't know how her song would affect Seru. Hmm, maybe if she... it would sting, but hopefully it would work. She yanked a few of her feathers from her wing with a wince and handed them back to Seru. "Plug your ears."

He gave her a look that the bizarre request deserved, but didn't question it amid a fight. Seru did his best to stuff the fluff from the proffered feathers into his ears as they beat as hasty a retreat as they could manage, backpedaling toward the other side.

Their options remained limited until they were both clear and the enemy closer. The last thing they needed was the bridge catching fire while they were still on it.

Thalasia listened for him to move. She didn't back up any further than the edge of the bridge. The technique she used on the guiler from the previous day may not work for these two, but a siren's song was adjustable. Opening her mouth, she executed a darker aria and used the melody to intensify the wind around the two guilers.

It whipped around each creature like a hurricane and sandstorm barreling down on them all at once. The waves from the ocean responded in force, raging against the shore. Both of the guilers attempted to react, but neither could fight the strength of the wind.

The wild energy emanating from Seru settled just as she sent their two foes sprawling. "Nicely done," he commended.

With the song finished and their enemy swept away, she glanced over at him and smiled. His appreciation for her ability distracted her from the way her heart pounded and her pulse raced. Her third eye opened before she had the chance to look away. Thalasia's eyes rolled into the back of her head until nothing but white could be seen. Her knees buckled, but before she hit the ground she had the sense of a pair of arms coming around her body.

Without warning, Thalasia collapsed. Seru reached out and caught her fall.

"Thalasia," he called. "Are you alright?"

When she didn't respond, he lifted her in his arms, surprised at how light she was. Momentarily, he wondered if—like most birds—her bones were hollow. He carried her across the bridge and thought back to the sight of her song. He'd only read a few cryptic myths and legends regarding the siren song. The opportunity to bear witness to the phenomenon was truly extraordinary. The strength and poetic nature of the ability proved far superior to what texts had described.

As they approached the other side, Thalasia stirred. Her body stiffened as she rested a hand against Seru's chest. "You can put me down now, please."

Seru nodded, gingerly setting Thalasia on her feet. Though he made certain to linger within arm's reach until he was sure she was steady. "Are you alright?"

It didn't take too much for her to gain her balance. Her gaze swung away from him and toward the sun. "Yes, I'm fine, thank you."

He couldn't help but be amused. As he plucked the feathers from his ears, he allowed his curiosity to get the better of him, hoping to distract her. "Your song worked wonders on those guilers. Can you do that anytime you want? Or are there certain... prerequisites?" he asked, offering her what remained of the blue quills.

Quietly accepting the quills, Thalasia turned to the bridge's banister. She opened her hand and released the quills into the water. "Any time I want. I acclimate the song to the situation by altering the notes and undertones based on what I need."

"That must take a tremendous amount of skill."

Thalasia shrugged off the comment. "I learned at a very young age how to control my voice."

"Perhaps you can offer a spot of advice to the young matriarch," Seru said, sounding a tad uneasy. "She's likely to give us both a lashing upon our return. Thank you. Your quick thinking saved us." He rubbed his ears, which were still ringing slightly.

Peering at him for the first time since he'd set her on her own two feet, Thalasia smirked. "I don't think she'd care too much for my advice." Her nose wrinkled with a brief wince. "Sorry about that. I guess feathers aren't the best barriers."

"Not your fault," he replied. "Now we know for the next time. We'll be better prepared." He glanced down the remaining stretch of bridge, back towards Prisma Isle. "We'd best report in. Preferably before the Regina loses her head." He extended a hand toward Thalasia.

Tilting her head, she studied Seru for a moment. Thalasia opened her mouth and snapped it shut. She exhaled a deep breath. "Thank you." With a curt nod, she steeled her shoulders and let the unspoken remain in the air as she walked toward Prisma Isle.

"Thalasia..." Seru called after her. "If you ever wish to... get anything off your chest, or simply care to talk, I hope you know that I'll gladly listen and offer my assistance in any way I can. We're in this together. Whether by choice or destiny's demand."

She stopped in her tracks and looked back at him. "I wish it was that simple, but experience has taught me otherwise."

A tightness around his eyes said he understood. The offer stood. "I'm sure our new Matriarch's brash accusations have only enforced that. And while I realize my apology in her stead is but a shadow of what's truly deserved, I offer it. You don't strike me as a true enemy here. Sadly, our culture has led us to be wary of strangers and to strike first rather than wait to be betrayed. You've caught the worst of that since your arrival. I know it's still early in our venture, but I hope in time we can learn to trust and confide in one another. My offer will remain open until you're ready."

Thalasia blinked, and a small sigh escaped. "I appreciate it, as well as your need to apologize on her behalf. But she's not the first to accuse me of something. One gets accustomed to the ill-laid blame when they stand out like I do. I've learned it comes with the territory."

"So, it's true, then... that most of your kind aren't as vibrantly and beautifully colored as you?" Seru inquired. "Even here, sirens are a rarity. Much like us, they choose to keep to themselves, barring the odd trade deal or political envoy."

"Yes, that's true." She tugged at the hem of her tank top and readjusted it again. "I don't look anything like my parents. I believe they were closer to what every other siren looks like."

"Your coloring might be unusual, Thalasia, but it isn't something you should be ashamed of." He placed a gentle hand on her shoulder to still her self-conscious fidgeting. A hand on the now-cool metal collar, he continued, the artfully inscribed glyphs dictating the terms of his imprisonment glistening in the low light reflecting off the water's surface. "I'm not at all like the rest, either. I know much of that is easier said than done. You shouldn't allow others to determine your value; instead, allow it to be their undoing. Their underestimation of you and your value serves you more than you know."

Her silver eyes sparkled as her gaze danced over the minute details of the collar. "Have you ever wondered what your life would be like without that thing?"

Seru offered a bitter smile. "Every second of every day. Though I also fear the day it finally comes off... when my true nature is set free, I'm uncertain I'll still be the same me. I can't help but wonder how much of this careful control belongs to the former Matriarch's intricate bindings and how much is my own."

"You don't know that. If you're not in control, then you have no way of knowing your true self," Thalasia said. She tentatively reached up to the collar and scrutinized its nuances. "I'd like to help you get this off. One of us deserves freedom."

"I was born of malicious desire to destroy," Seru replied. "Sadly, that doesn't leave much room for..." He pinched the bridge of his nose. He hadn't intended to go this in depth. He shook his head as if to clear it, a smile shining through. "Forgive me, Thalasia," he said. "I intended to be of some assistance to you, but I seem to take advantage of your kindness. Truly, I appreciate the offer. And I hope I can one day return the favor. However, I believe we have more pressing and troubling matters to tend to first."

"For the record, you can't help with my tether. It comes at a sacrifice and I've accepted it." Thalasia swallowed, carefully regarding him before she took a step back and put some space between them. "But you're right. We have more pressing matters."

Chapter Three

Aurelia paced the beach, halting as the pair came within earshot. Her taloned hands found their way to her hips as they drew closer. She wore a ferocious scowl. Heat rolled off her in waves, each one burning slightly more than the last.

The guards at her back sweated in silence, sure to remain in position while maintaining a safe distance from Aurelia's easy-bake frenzy.

Seru cringed. The young ruler clearly wasn't happy. "You'd best let me go first," he whispered to Thalasia.

Thalasia nodded, her shoulders tense as she laced her fingers together at the small of her back, whatever wall she'd let down clearly back in place. "Sure. I'm not really in the mood for her antics, anyway."

"Her roar is worse than her bite," Seru offered. "Most of the time."

"Did you find anything out about our enemy, or did you simply take your sweet time serenading one another?" Aurelia snapped, sensing a shift in both of them.

Seru chuckled despite his best efforts. "No, Majesty," he responded. "I'm afraid our little scrimmage with the initial guiler's companions left me... off balance. Thalasia was generous enough to slow her pace to accommodate me."

Thalasia's body went completely still as her eyebrows furrowed at Seru's statement. Her response only lasted for a second.

Aurelia squinted at him, her gaze boring into him with her startling violet eyes. She didn't buy it. But she also didn't know what to say to such an admission, especially in the presence of her army. Seru already had a target on his back. It escaped her why he'd openly invite further ridicule from their kinsmen.

She'd felt the spike in energy when his beast surfaced, sensed his distress the moment the magic seized him. She bit her lower lip, uncertain how to address the issue without drawing further attention to his weakened state.

Taking her silence as acceptance, Seru continued, bringing Aurelia up to speed with the vanished body and two elemental combatants Thalasia had swiftly dispatched.

Aurelia followed Seru's story intently. She barely spared Thalasia a glance until the very end. Her eyes darting between Seru and the siren, she spoke in hushed whispers, confirming she'd heard him correctly.

Canting her head, Thalasia leaned against the bridge's banister and crossed one ankle over the other. "Ask me a question if necessary. Otherwise, we should get moving."

Aurelia bared teeth as she spoke to Thalasia. "Don't worry, siren, you'll get your turn."

Returning to the wall of gilded fighters, she instructed them to hold their post. If they sighted any guilers, they were to be killed without question as soon as they left Candescent Isle. With Seru by her side, she strode over to the siren's perch. "You'll talk as we walk, while I tend to Seru's binding," she told the woman through a show of teeth. "If your story doesn't align with his, I'll know one of you is lying."

Thalasia barked out in laughter and started walking toward the forest. "You're funny, dragon-girl. I thought you were a ruler, not an interrogator. But if you really need a reiteration of the facts, here it is: I sent the bad guys flying away. The end."

"Sometimes being a good ruler means donning multiple hats," Aurelia stated, her hands and the golden aura emitting from them finding Seru's collar as he adjusted the fabric. "I don't trust you, and as much as I adore my Regent, he has a tendency to manipulate the facts in whatever way best suits him in the moment. So is the nature of politics... and war. Survival," she amended with a frown. Some distant memory playing behind her eyes. "I'll never get the whole truth, no matter how honest the two parties are. But I'll hear your side in full."

"Please oblige her, Thalasia," Seru requested, calm as could be. If he'd told Aurelia another tale, he didn't betray it.

Thalasia stopped, crossed her arms, and rolled her eyes at Seru. "For fuck's sake, fine. We walked over, noticed someone had removed the body, and spotted the two guilers in the distance. He did his thing, I did mine, and when it all settled, we headed back. Satisfied?"

"So, you lost the body and created two more... that you left behind without inspecting for clues?" Aurelia asked. "If you were just going to turn back at the first signs of danger, I could have gone myself and saved you both the trouble."

"We erred on the side of caution, Regina. Without a definite number, approaching their shores seemed unwise," Seru interjected. "Especially considering my condition. Do not blame Thalasia for an unpredictable variable we introduced."

Aurelia heaved a sigh, pressing in closer to better see the illuminated glyphs etched into Seru's collar as she continued to manipulate their magic.

Bearing a frown, Thalasia groaned. "I didn't lose the body. Although it was gone, I could still see some of its blood in the sand. As for the other two, we wouldn't have been able to search for them. Their bodies were more likely in parts scattered between the shore and water. I wouldn't have taken that risk with his life, especially with that *thing* around his neck." She shot Seru an apologetic look, then flicked her eyes toward Candescent Isle. "For all we know, they can come across without using the bridge. So, if you're done assaulting our decisions, then we best move on."

Seru let out a startled yelp as the energy feeding into the metal misfired.

Thalasia's fists balled up.

"Sorry, sorry..." Aurelia apologized, choosing another channel for her magic to explore.

"Thalasia isn't wrong." He slipped a few talons between the warm metal and his throat.

Aurelia always did her best, but it was an unpredictable contraption, far more complex than even the most skilled locksmith could navigate. "The entire fleet is on standby should that occur," she said, feeling for just the right connection within the collar. When her golden energy found the former Matriarch's silver, the two momentarily warred for dominance before fusing and smoothing out. If she pushed too hard, the device either constricted and choked him, or it burned or zapped him with the reactive magical energy flowing inside it. "Better?"

"For now." Seru grimaced as she pulled back. "Thank you."

The tension in the siren's body ebbed as the situation with the collar resolved.

"Don't mention it." Aurelia helped him adjust it to his comfort. "We should make our way toward the town. The one with the market, where most of the earthbound conduct their trade," Aurelia stated, hoping Seru's near-perfect memory served him better. "That way we can question most of the species, then branch out from there. But first..."

Aurelia slipped the straps of her dress over her shoulders. "We need to change. And you"—She reached into the knapsack Seru had brought her, producing a cloak and set of riding boots and tossing them to Thalasia—"need to cover those wings and talons."

She caught the boots and cloak without issue. Raising an eyebrow at Aurelia, Thalasia smirked, tossed the boots back at her, and draped the cloak over her shoulders. "You don't get to town much, do you? If I am correct about Prisma Isle, then my talons will not be an issue."

Aurelia let the boots fall at her feet. "Fine. Suit yourself, chicken legs." She stripped and changed out in the open.

Seru reluctantly followed suit.

Most dragons, or any shifter really, didn't mind exposing their bodies, even in human form. Most chose loose-fitting garments for a similar reason. Restricted movement didn't sit well with them.

Aurelia's eyes wandered over Seru's roadmap of scars, as they always did. Some were obviously lashings from his mother's whip. The rest were battle scars from the Great War and the subsequent destruction of his brothers. He caught her stare, but as their eyes met, she didn't look away. They were far too familiar with one another for that. Instead, she stuck out her tongue in a quick flash of fangs, drawing a laugh from her self-conscious friend as he shook his head.

Aurelia spotted Thalasia's wide eyes locked on the scars on Seru's back, and the bird-girl spun on the back of her heel as if embarrassed to be taking in what she must see as an intimate scene. Her shoulders dropped next, and she walked a short distance away as if to put some distance between her and them.

"What's the matter, siren? Don't see anything you like? Are the androgynous more your style?"

Seru tensed at Aurelia's question. "Majesty, I don't think those are appropriate questions."

"Why not? Surely, she's got a preference?" Aurelia frowned.

Clearing his throat, Seru tried again. "Most, if not all, sirens are female, Aurelia. Their options are limited with selecting a mate. It may be a delicate subject."

The infomercial did little to deter her. "That's ridiculous. Just because they can't produce offspring doesn't mean they can't have sex."

Seru looked at Thalasia apologetically.

"I wonder... do sirens have feathers down there, too?"

"Did he?" Seru growled, a last attempt at ending the conversation.

Aurelia paused, searching her memories. "You know," she said, bemused. "I don't actually recall. If we ever cross paths, I'll be sure to inform you. After I've killed him."

Her body rigid, Thalasia said nothing as she balled up her fists. Clenching her jaw, she removed the cloak, allowing it to fall to the ground. She unzipped the back of her tank top and dropped it, revealing multiple scars on her back, including two jagged white slashes, one on each shoulder blade close to her wings. She didn't hide the swell of her breasts but remained there for a moment so they could clearly see the breadth of what she'd endured. Without bothering to cover herself back up, she took off into the air and flew toward the forest.

Seru gave Aurelia the venomous look she'd earned.

"They weren't any worse than yours," she offered, shrugging on the last of her new clothes.

"You don't know what she's survived, Aurelia. You had no right to assume and assault her that way."

Aurelia rolled her eyes in response. "Why are you both being so dramatic?"

Shaking his head because her response disgusted him and her unwillingness to comprehend what her smarting off had cost Thalasia, Seru dared to test the new interworking of his collar and transformed into, not a dragon, but a small cluster of storm clouds.

"Thalasia ..." Seru called.

Tugging her shirt back in place on the perch she'd found, Thalasia closed her eyes and sighed. Why did he have to follow her? She hadn't meant to share her wounds that way... better yet, not at all. Her walls had been in place for years. It was safer, not just for her, but also for those around her.

In a short time, she'd discovered in him, kin. She found in him someone who understood the horrors she had endured, the resulting loneliness, and the cage that trapped her. Opening her eyes, she stared out across the plush forest. "Please, go away."

Following the sound of her voice, Seru stopped just beneath the towering tree she'd selected as her hiding place. "I won't do you the injustice of apologizing for her. You deserve better. What she said was cruel. She doesn't understand..." he trailed off. "I don't mean that as an excuse. The Regina has been confined to the Clouds all her life. There is kindness in her heart, but it's something she's been taught rigorously to bury." He paused. "If you wish to be alone, I'm afraid I can't award you that. It's too dangerous. But if you will permit silence, it's my turn to oblige."

Oh, she gathered how little dragon-girl understood. Not just about sirens, but about life. No, it wasn't an excuse, and of course, she had witnessed the young dragon to be kind. To him. But that wasn't the problem, was it? She could handle the girl's snarky attitude. Even work with it, *if* it came down to it. The problem was, it wouldn't be fair to blame him. Nor was it his fault. It was hers. It was her history that closed her off, and her walls that had cracked. Undoing her braid, Thalasia ran her fingers through her sapphire blue hair and proceeded to re-braid her locks. "I'm safer alone."

"No one's safe alone, Thalasia," Seru said, settling beneath the tree. "Not even someone as powerful as you."

Thalasia paused mid-braid. She was going to have to tell him. Make him see the truth. She didn't want compassion or empathy. She just wanted to finish her job, to complete the tasks Demeter had laid before her eyes. Slipping the band around her wrist, Thalasia hopped from the branch and drifted to the ground. "You don't get it. I didn't pass out. I had a vision. *That* got me these scars. A shape shifter found out about me and decided I'd be useful to her. When I refused, she beat me until that stopped working, then she went for my wings. I'm alive because of one of her guards. He sacrificed his life for mine. I won't take that risk. I will not lose someone else because of my abilities."

Seru craned his neck to gaze into her eyes as he spoke. "By that logic, you risking your life for mine earlier was a mistake."

He was wrong. So wrong. In that moment, she'd made a decision, and it was one she intended to see through. Thalasia shook her head, her half-braid falling loose. "It was what needed to happen. I will see the mission I was given here through, and I will keep my promise to you. When that's done, so am I. I have nothing to tether me to this world. No mate, no children... and I see neither in my future. I will do what needs to be done."

Seru cocked his head in question. "Your extra sight may show you many things, but it doesn't show you all. Don't give up on this life, or yourself, that easily."

He stood, gently taking her hands in his. "I, for one, don't intend to. Nor do I intend to allow you to condemn yourself to a lifetime of heartache and misery. I believe that guard friend of yours would agree that it would be a terrible waste, especially for one so young, so lovely, and with such a generous heart."

It wasn't giving up. It was making a choice. Why couldn't he see that? Because he was too close. Just like her parents. Just like Klaus. Removing her hands from his, Thalasia took a step back. "You fear what it'll be like with your collar off. I fear what would happen if I let my walls go completely down. I won't see you as a prisoner, but I won't remain one either."

"That's twice today I've attempted to comfort you... and it's twice I've failed," he admitted, his voice low.

She grimaced. It caused her heart physical pain to see him so dejected, especially when he wasn't to blame. Thalasia swallowed and dropped her gaze to her hands. Before her mind could catch up to her body's decision, she closed the distance between the two of them and hugged him. "Please don't think this is your failure. It belongs to me."

Seru startled. After a moment, he returned her embrace, careful of her wings and of his own strength. Her blue hair tickled his nose as he dipped his chin over the curve of her neck. "Thank you, Thalasia."

Of their own accord, her wings came around them like a cocoon. Her breath caught in the back of her throat. What was her body doing? Nothing like this had ever happened before. Although, maybe it was being so close to a male. No, she'd been around men. It didn't make sense. But she didn't dare examine the desire too closely, otherwise it might be her undoing. "No thanks necessary, Seru."

Someone cleared their throat from beneath a nearby tree. "You both realize that your cross-species kids would be massive scaly feathery disasters, right? If you're done playing out your tragic soap opera, can we get hopping and skipping that way?" Dragon-girl pointed in the proper direction. "Your fancy map says the central market city is that way. If you're lucky, they might even have a chapel," she added, striding off.

Thalasia's wings retracted, and she stepped out of Seru's hold. Her eyes narrowed at the dragon-girl. Up to this point, she'd met her snark head on. Perhaps it was time she took another approach altogether. Exhaling a deep breath, Thalasia crossed her arms.

"No." She held up a hand to stop Seru from interjecting. "I get it, dragon-girl. You and I obviously don't like each other. Nor do we trust one another. You know nothing about my species, and my knowledge of yours is little. We don't know a thing about the other or what we've been through in our lives. As far as I'm concerned, that doesn't need to change, but we need to respect one another in order to work together. So, how about you and I start over?"

Uncrossing her arms, Thalasia held out her hand for the other woman. She'd extended a branch; it was up to the dragon-girl to take it.

Dragon-girl turned back just enough to cock an eyebrow at Thalasia and her outstretched palm before turning to Seru.

He stood with his arms crossed, almost as if he were hugging himself in her absence, coveting the warmth. His wounded but firm eyes and stubborn stance said he wasn't moving and expected an answer as much as she did.

"Does it really mean that much to you?" the dragon-girl asked.

Seru's lip recoiled, exposing his fang. "Not if you don't mean it."

The young dragon-shifter threw her hands up, exasperated. "Why do I have to mean it? If you were in my shoes, you wouldn't."

He shook his head, his grip tightening on his arms. "If we were up there,"—He pointed overhead, beyond the canopies, indicating the Clouds—"you're exactly right. I'd do whatever was necessary to make peace, to survive, as I have under both your rule and Hers. But we aren't up there. I'm not playing a role for the Court, where the wrong answer, the wrong turn of phrase earns me a gilded spear to the gut or a thousand years of agony with this thing wrapped around my throat! You gave me hope when you said you wanted to change the way the Clouds were run, make it so each dragon under your care had a voice." He took a moment to steady his rising tone. "If those words were hollow, and *this*,"—He swept a hand over her person—"these cruel words and thoughtless, self-serving demands are who you really are? You're no better than Her. You are Her. Worse."

Seru turned away, unable to hold the dragon-shifter's gaze.

Thalasia kept her hand out, although she had nearly lowered it several times. At this rate, the dragon-girl might never agree. Seeing Seru seethe with anger, when only moments ago the world had been calm, was like a stab to the wing. Thalasia reached out and squeezed his arm. If he had been anyone else, she might've used her abilities to soothe him, but she wouldn't do that. She just hoped the small touch would be enough.

Flicking her eyes back to the young Matriarch, Thalasia sighed. "I know your heart isn't as black as you make it out to be. I've seen it in the way you care for him. So, if you won't do it for yourself or the mission, then do it for him." With her one hand still outstretched, she nodded to Seru.

"Fine." the dragon-girl announced, voice thick with punished tears. Reluctantly extending a hand, she took hold of Thalasia's. One firm hand-shake and she withdrew. "But at the end of this, it seems you have a choice to make as well." She turned and walked toward the town, sure to keep her back to them both as she led the way.

Thalasia groaned. It was better than nothing. It might've been nice to know the dragon-girl's name, but she'd accept what little the female had given. This wasn't the only mission on her plate. She turned to Seru. "I need to go back for the cloak. I'll return in a moment."

"Leave it"—He shifted out of his and draped it over her shoulders with a heavy sigh. "Between the effort with Aurelia and this"—He thumbed his collar—"we've wasted far too much time already."

Valid point. Not that she'd helped in the matter.

He sounded exhausted. With a strained smile, he offered his hand to Thalasia. "Call it childish, but after all that, I'm feeling a little petty."

Raising an eyebrow at his hand, a small smile curled on her lips. It probably wasn't the wisest idea, but she couldn't stop herself. Thalasia placed her hand in his and gave it a quick squeeze. "May I ease your muscles as we walk?"

"I appreciate it," Seru said, "but I don't want to hurt you accidentally. When my emotions aren't subdued, the electricity generated isn't friend-ly—no matter how well intended. I'll be alright, I just need to secure a room once we get to town. You're more than welcome to accompany me should you need rest."

"I don't think you could ever hurt me, but I trust your judgment." Though, perhaps it was for the best. She didn't want to remember the happier time, a time when she had hope for her future, especially with what she'd decided. The past needed to remain buried where it belonged. She had to think of what remained. "Yes, I would like to join you."

Chapter Four

Seru watched as Aurelia negotiated with the burly cook for salmon from his grill for the tiny purple gemstone ring on her pinky finger.

Aurelia held her hand up with wide eyes. She obligingly slipped the band from her finger, sparing a glance to Seru.

He nodded his consent, his arm looped around Thalasia's waist so he wouldn't lose her in the crowd. He wasn't about to step between Aurelia's eager excitement and food to teach her the art of bartering.

Aurelia bounced on her toes, thrusting the jewelry at the man with a toothy grin. "Deal."

Thalasia's fists clenched as she peered over each shoulder, her silver eyes watching the passersby glancing from stall to stall. An array of colored awnings decorated stalls boasting wares from all over the isle. Her gaze flicked back to the vendor as she shoved her hands into the front pockets of her capris and whispered to Seru, "Have I ever mentioned how much I don't like crowds?"

"Once Aurelia has her fish, we can break off into the side streets to search for that room, if you prefer?" he offered in a hushed whisper.

Thalasia nodded. Although she kept her hands tucked into the pockets of her pants, her fingers tapped nervously against her clothed thighs as her eyes flitted around the market.

A twitch of a smile lit Seru's face as he watched the Matriarch *negotiate* and regale the sweaty dwarf of their appetites.

With some reluctance, he allowed her to swindle him out of every filet he had on the grill. She left the man flustered, no doubt amazed at her ability to sling the haul over her shoulder with ease.

"Want something else?" Aurelia asked, more to Seru than Thalasia.

She was clearly enjoying the festivities, and he hated to dim her shine. It was the first time over the last two days of their journey she'd truly smiled. "I think we're going to secure accommodations for the night," he said, turning to find the indicator for lodgings off the main strip.

"You're welcome to join us," he quickly added as her face fell. "Or stay and enjoy the market. Just try not to part with too many valuables too, obviously." Seru caught her by the wrist. "Remember, we don't want to draw attention."

"Yeah, yeah... okay." Aurelia shook her arm free and rolled her eyes at his words of caution before turning to venture back into the fray.

Inhaling and exhaling a couple of deep breaths, Thalasia closed her eyes for a moment. Opening her eyes, she glanced around, and then peered at Seru before turning her attention back to the market. Much more relaxed than she had been a second ago, she asked, "Do you think we could find a place for clothes first?"

Seru watched Thalasia intently as she calmed herself, surprised by her efficiency and self-discipline. He raised an eyebrow at the request, but consented with little fuss. "Whatever the lady wishes." He smiled down at her. "Any place catch your eye?"

"While this is my general go-to, it won't quite do for..." She gestured toward the sky to indicate Pteryrina, home of the Sirens. "And I'd really prefer not to have to come back here."

He nodded before sweeping an arm to clear the way. "After you."

Hesitant, she stepped further into the bustling crowd, careful to keep her wings tucked in tight beneath the cloak. Her eyes scanned the local store fronts as they passed a variety of species. A mermaid selling seashell trinkets. A djinn dancing barefoot to a satyr's flute, its face concealed behind a sheer veil. An amphibian fisherman duo offered fresh filets of fish and odd baubles raised from the deep of local lakes and rivers, each with a tale attached. A canine laid out foraged herbs, nuts, and berries of all shapes, colors, and textures in woven sacks.

They continued past buildings that lined the way, comprising an inn and tavern, a music shop, and a karaoke bar named Zancle's Rock. She smirked at the name and followed one of the rickety road signs pointing toward a lake and clothing boutique.

Seru trailed just behind her, observing the multicultural mob they waded through. There were small clusters of major species, but most individuals registered as unique. He didn't remember so much variety existing during the war. The earthbound had been busy in bringing about their world of peace and commingling. Luckily, that allowed them to blend right in.

He traced Thalasia's gaze to the karaoke bar, a curious choice but not out of the realm for a siren—especially for one with a voice like hers. How was an establishment like Zancle's Rock run and what happened when the patrons' vocal battles got out of hand? He cringed inwardly.

With a quick nod to Seru, Thalasia stopped in front of a small shop and stepped through the doorway. The chime on the door Thalasia pushed through brought his attention to their destination. He filed in behind her, his eyes taking in every detail.

Her eyes drank in the boutique from the various gowns, suits, and everyday items hanging in many places. Instead of going straight for what would've been her preference, Thalasia headed over to the gowns. She perused them until she found a white flowing dress that tied at the shoulders, had a deep V neckline, a low scoop back, and a silver belt.

Seru stayed by the door, his eyes focused on the curtain behind the counter. He kept Thalasia in his periphery as he took a few steps forward. The champagne fabric shifted, but no one appeared.

His hackles rose. Someone was watching them. "Thalasia... get what you need and let's go." He didn't like it here. Didn't like the sudden, barely spiked anxiety. His eyes wandered over the shelves behind the counter, along some folded fabrics, and around a few books. Nothing was amiss. A large orb with the sheen of a pearl rested within a delicate metal sculpture. It distorted his reflection and gave off a strange aura.

Thalasia nodded. She swept quickly through the boutique and collected two more items. Once done, she went to the front counter and laid all three items on it. "Hello?" Thalasia called out as she reached into the inside pocket of her pants and removed a tiny purple pouch.

The sweet scent of lotus blossoms filled the air. A mist seeped into the boutique from beneath the door.

Appearing out of nowhere, the shop owner spooked Seru and slipped past Thalasia unseen. "What a lovely choice, miss. It's certain to sweep your intended off their feet, revealing what's directly in front of you."

Before she responded, it turned its attention toward Seru. "My, my... what exquisite color-changing scales. You must be the last of little Verie's saint beasts. The last remnants of her still clinging to this world, if I'm not mistaken. It's an honor... almost as captivating as the blue feathers on your siren friend."

Thalasia gasped, shuffling back from the counter. She clutched the tiny purple pouch to her chest. "But..."

It spared her a glance out of the corner of its eye and continued on as if no disruption existed. Its gaze swung back to Seru. "What a treat to have two such rarities enter my shop on this most unexpected of days. Truly a blessing from the gods."

Unnerved that the strange, ancient creature could see through him, Seru blinked. The perfume intoxicating the air in the enclosed space became hard to breathe. Agitated, he backed into the door like a serpent coiling in on itself, his fangs bared in a desperate, fearsome display, the chime creating narrowed slits in those stormy eyes.

"She was so fond of discarding the parts of herself that she didn't care for. You, however, are the crown jewel of all her misguided efforts," it stated, almost as if reminiscing about a time long past. But clearly, its memories remained as vivid as if they had happened yesterday. "A fragment of the former Matriarch given flesh. All that rage, all that hatred, molded into such a magnificent monster of destruction. And so close to being set free..."

Seru's fractured collar emitted a bright silvery glow amid the golden glyphs. The creature appeared to take delight in his unbidden response. It had to be casting a spell, something slowly raising his beast from the depths.

Whatever magic had held fast to the door to the boutique released. A startling electricity infused in the air, sparkling along their exposed flesh, raising hairs, feathers, and even the threads on the fabric of their clothing. Seru bolted as soon as the door opened.

The shop owner stood there unphased, hands clasped neatly behind him, while sporting an unnerving smile. "I do so look forward to your next visit."

Unsure of what had just occurred, Thalasia stood there speechless as she stared at the closed door. Nothing she'd done seemed to register for Seru. Her gaze drifted to the shop owner. She hissed at the creature and ran off after Seru.

He darted so quickly through the crowd that she nearly lost sight of him several times as he ran aimlessly across the maze of rickety bridges. There didn't appear to be any focus in his direction.

She chased after him as best she could. Free of the crowd, her heart raced beneath her chest as she spotted him rubbing his arms crouched down by the water's edge. His breath fogged with the mist in short, quick bursts. He ground his jaw.

Clasping the pouch in her hands, her brows drew together. Thalasia approached him gently, sure to keep some distance between them. His earlier warning replayed in her mind. As much as she wanted to reach out to him, she didn't dare stray too far from his concern. "Seru?"

With a deep growl and his fangs extended, he snapped at her. Dark clouds churned behind his white eyes. His shoulders slumped as recognition seemed to set in. "Please... stay back."

Without the chance to even give him that, Seru shot to his feet and took off again.

This time, she didn't chase after him. Giving him space, she let him go and dropped to her knees, her body giving way to the vision that sat on the edge for the last minute.

In her mind, she saw the same green-winged siren she'd seen upon her arrival appear. As well as a small village of guilers ... and smoke. As quickly as it appeared, the images left.

Slouching, Thalasia allowed the tears to fall. She didn't need to hide them. She was alone. And she deserved to be.

It was her fault.

He'd gone with her to the shop at her request. It had been to appease her. She was to blame.

For all of it.

She had to truly let him go. He'd be better off without her.

Thalasia sat back on her feet and wiped the tears away. It would be difficult, but she could keep him at arm's length until they went their separate ways. It was the best way to keep him safe... at least until she freed him for good.

Then everything would be finished, including the curse she brought upon good people.

Cleaning the rest of her face, Thalasia stood and headed for the inn. A few things had come of this, but the price hadn't been worth it. She weaved across several bridges, avoiding people as much as possible.

She arrived at the inn and hardly took notice of the innkeeper's species. It wasn't important for the task at hand.

"Good afternoon, Miss...?"

"Thalasia," she replied automatically.

"Oh! Yes, yes. We have your room all prepared."

None of the words that left the dainty young man's mouth passed her ears. She didn't need to know any of that. All she cared about was where Seru had ended up. She'd given him the privacy he asked for, but she wouldn't leave him alone. She couldn't. Not when they could've avoided the situation twice over.

If they hadn't gone to the store. If they'd left when he expressed his unease. She'd been selfish in her actions and Seru had paid for her decision.

Thalasia blinked at the key presented to her by the innkeeper. Oh, right. She clasped her hand around his and hummed a light tune. Locking eyes with the young creature, she continued the song until his gaze swirled, indicating a successful manipulation. "What room is Seru, my gentleman friend, in?"

"Second floor, two-oh-seven, at the end of the hallway."

"Thank you." She collected the key she'd been given for her room and headed up the staircase to the second floor. Her shoulders sagged as she approached his room. She touched the door briefly and slumped to the floor.

Tucking her legs in close, Thalasia rested her head on top of her knees. Releasing a heavy sigh, the weight of the last two days dragged her down and pulled her into a restless sleep.

Aurelia smiled at the small band of children, her violet eyes intent on following their demonstration. A young faun leaped gayly about a series of geometric markings etched in the soil while her trio of friends rolled a handful of bejeweled dice to determine their task and place.

The colorful dice skittered across cobbles before rebounding off the nearby fountain. The amphibious boy hopped the shapes depicted on the winking dice face. As he positioned himself behind the faun, he readied himself, crouching low before springing clear over her antlers. The children all squealed in delight.

A mangy feline, fur hopping with fleas, collected the dice, raced over to the dragon-shifter, and pressed them into her palm. The scratchy kitten bounced with glee as Aurelia's dice yielded a seven-prong star. "What does that mean?"

As the question escaped her lips, a static sizzled over her skin. She straightened abruptly, head jerking to see if she could spot Seru among the crowd. Something had distressed him. He needed her. Or else the saint beast would soon level this peaceful market, making it the first appearance since the war.

War would surely explode if anyone discovered Seru alive.

She leaned up on tiptoe and attempted to peer around the taller townspeople with little success. The eager kitten tugged at the hem of her dress, pointing to the seven-pointed star atop the roof. Aurelia craned her head, shielding her gaze from the intensity of the sun. Her eyes found a slew of barrels beside the building. Using the edge of the fountain as a stepping stone, she cloud-stepped from the ledge of the barrels, swung from the sign proclaiming the abandoned building a church, and somersaulted to the rooftop, garnering herself applause and praise from the children and a better vantage point.

Steadying herself on the starry spire, she easily spotted a shape she thought to be Seru fleeing across the main strip before disappearing down an alleyway. She searched his path and found no sight of Thalasia. With a curse, Aurelia jumped down. Startled gasps from passersby did little to deter her. She left her day's haul and what remained of the cooked fish to her tiny admirers and raced after Seru.

When she finally discovered Seru's hiding spot—an inconspicuous inn called the Flight of Fancy—the static had turned to tiny currents lashing out to bite her the closer she came. She captured a glimpse of Thalasia at the counter. Apparently, the bluebird had chased him down as well, but how much had she seen? Did she cause Seru to lose control of his beast, or had the collar malfunctioned once more? The subtle scent of lotus blossoms caused her scales to stand on end.

She knew where they'd been... *Meraki*, home to a skinchanger renowned for his *sight* and ability to unmask disguises almost as well as he crafted the continent's finest magically—imbued clothing. Had the two of them taken her suggestion seriously?

With a disgruntled snort, Aurelia wove around the side of the inn and gained entrance to Seru's room without catching the siren's attention. She didn't have time for another fight or one of the bird-girl's sarcastic rants. She needed to get to her regent before his control slipped beyond the point of no return.

Aurelia cast a look quickly down both directions of the narrow alley before cloud-stepping her way to the open window on the second floor. She glided effortlessly through, finding his scarred form shivering atop a strange length of pillow on a wooden frame. She approached with caution, slow and steady, though he no doubt sensed her presence long before her outstretched palm brushed against his skin.

His hand immediately found hers, clasping it tighter than she would have liked. However, he didn't turn to greet her. It seemed to take every bit of focus he had to soothe his beast into pressing itself around the walls of his skin. Not unlike a cat leaning into its master in search of affection, though the beast instead searched for a way out, an opportunity to break free of its humanoid prison and return to the world.

The serpentine creature slowed its hunt for freedom at her touch. She disrobed and curled her form around his arched back, wrapping herself around his significantly larger frame as much as possible. She allowed her radiant power to manifest, and a soft glow soon intensified until every vein illuminated with golden light flowing from her into him.

Seru shuddered as the power cloaked him. A pained rumble vibrated through him as his overactive muscles turned from liquid to solid and retook their proper form. Each wave of power eased the tension in him, a gentle ebb and flow.

After a time, exhaustion claimed the saint beast. Aurelia eased up on her expenditure of power a little at a time until she could feel his heart beating steady within his massive chest.

Reclaiming her gown, she marched over to the door, where a shadow eclipsed the light filtering in from the oil lamps in the hall. She unceremoniously jerked the shoddy wooden slab open.

Thalasia's eyes opened wide as she caught herself from falling. Wringing her hands together, her gaze flicked from Aurelia to Seru. "Is he okay? Tell me he's okay."

"Are *you* feeling okay?" Aurelia asked incredulously. She hadn't expected the woman to be a nervous, fidgeting mess. With a roll of her eyes, she stepped aside, tossing her head in his direction. "He's fine. See for yourself."

Offering a brief appreciative nod, Thalasia rushed across the room. She kneeled down on the ground beside the bed and gently stroked Seru's cheek.

He twitched in his sleep, exposing prominent fangs in response to her touch before resettling.

"Sure you want to do that?" Her hands dropped to her hips. Bluebird really was strange. She couldn't decide if the girl was fearless or reckless. "I said he was alright, not harmless."

"I'm not sure of a lot of things right now. But him..." The words fell off. Thalasia sat back on her feet and watched him for a moment before standing. Her shoulders sagged as a heavy sigh escaped her mouth. "I don't suppose you heard anything around the market."

Aurelia shrugged nonchalantly. "Oh, you know, just rumors of a bride and groom fleeing their fitting at the local watering hole. Take it you two lovebirds made a new friend of that many-faced shifter lording over Lake Lucent." Her eyes narrowed as she cast her gaze from some place out the window back to them. "Thinking I might pay that treacherous queen a visit."

Facing Aurelia, Thalasia tilted her head and blinked. "What? Bride and groom? I didn't..." As if Aurelia's words finally registered, she glanced back to Seru. Her cheeks flushed. "Oh, no... w ..." She sighed again. "If that's where the shopkeeper came from. I didn't even see it come in." Thalasia rubbed her temples. "Instead of thinking of revenge, why don't we check out Zancle's Rock? It'll likely be the best place to gain some information."

Chapter Five

"You're ruining the dress," Aurelia commented, rising to her feet, decked out in a glitzy purple dress and stilettos.

Thalasia cocked an eyebrow and glanced down at the glimmering tiny blue dress she had on, which barely peeked through the cloak over her shoulders. It looked fine to her. "How? Am I wearing it wrong?"

Aurelia gestured vaguely to the cloak. "It can't be helped unless you can play off those wings as part of the costume. Let's just hope your troll doesn't decide to get a case of the midnight munchies and go for a bite out of my regent while we're gone."

It wasn't her first choice either, but they had to blend with the crowd. Not that she was positive the cloak helped or hindered them. Thalasia snickered. "There isn't enough fabric in this dress to even make that possible. And the troll will be fine. I instructed him not to enter and not to let anyone in until my return."

"That's kinda the point. Learn to show some skin," Aurelia said, turning to follow the fading light back into the city streets, which were now painted a brilliant shade of orange.

"I'm not the kind to show skin." Even though that dress she'd chosen earlier would show plenty. It was common among sirens... or so she'd been told. And she'd worn a few others in the past that one might consider revealing, but she'd stick to her story.

Thalasia strode along the town streets, grateful it was a little less crowded this late in the day. Her gaze flicked from the emptier vendor stalls to

Aurelia. The girl was obviously comfortable in the tiny dress, almost as if it had been made for her.

Aurelia wandered the maze of side streets until they came to the main strip. A crowd had coalesced in the karaoke bar. A few villagers sauntered past on their way home.

Wow. She hadn't expected so many species hanging around the doors, eagerly awaiting the bar's opening. Satyrs, a handful of half-breed sirens, mermaids, and a few others she presumed were shapeshifters, but she couldn't say for sure. They could be hard to decipher in their humanoid form. Nearly all of them dressed for a night out. Or maybe they were fae. She really should've learned more about this realm.

The doors flew open as the last rays of the sun set below the horizon. A young woman with bright amber eyes and long crimson hair cascading down her back in waves stepped out with a troll directly behind her. She flashed a thousand-watt smile. "Let's get this party started!"

Aurelia bit her bottom lip as she rolled her shoulders, swaying from side to side, eventually bumping shoulders with the gawking Thalasia. "Loosen up. It's a party, not a death sentence. You heard the cardinal lady."

"I'm as loose as I can be, given the situation." Her heart wasn't racing. Her pulse hadn't sped up, despite the growing number of people. Thalasia stayed by Aurelia's side as they made their way inside, past the puke-green troll. She scanned over the high-top tables and located an empty one. Grabbing Aurelia's hand, she dragged her over to the table made from blue agate before anyone else claimed it. The dark wooden stools served as a perfect contrast to all the various shades of blue surrounding them.

Music filled the large, cavern-like building. The woman who had greeted the crowd earlier stood in a box to the right of the stage. "All right, you beautiful creatures, you know how this works. I got my sexy on, so come whisper in my ear what you'd like to sing."

"That'd be your cue." Aurelia clapped Thalasia on the shoulder. "I don't sing. Go use your siren wiles so we can get our answers. Knock out all the rest. I'm going to hit up the bar for drinks..." she faltered. "Or at least whatever swill these earthbound pawn off as drinks."

"I'm sorry. You want me to go up on stage? Are you out of your mind?" Her gaze narrowed. It would be a sure-fire way to get them discovered. She couldn't imagine a siren had stepped foot in this establishment before now.

Thalasia adjusted the cloak a bit as she climbed on the stool. It was getting stuffy.

Aurelia skittered to a halt, leaning on the tabletop to keep their conversation private. "You charmed the troll at the inn. Charming the crowd shouldn't be too difficult with all the fancy amplification equipment they've loaded this place with. That's the upside of being a pure-blood over a half-breed. We have all the power."

"You realize the second I open my mouth, they're going to know I'm a siren, which will make this cloak pointless." She didn't plan on singing. Thalasia glanced past Aurelia. Not to mention it looked like a couple of satyrs were already fighting over the stage.

"So, you just wanna sit here and listen to *that?*" Aurelia jerked a thumb toward the satyr pair, the disbelief and irritation in her voice obvious.

Thalasia stifled a laugh at the pair, who had settled in on the back-lit blue stone stage, and crooned out a horrible melody. "Do I want to listen to it? No, but it is kind of amusing."

"It also doesn't give us answers."

Damn. Aurelia was right. Thalasia's gaze flicked from the stage and back again. She didn't want to get on stage, but she might not have a choice either. They needed answers... a lot of them. "Go get some drinks and I'll think about it. See if you can order some food, too."

Aurelia rolled her eyes dramatically as she turned on her heel, marching up to the bar.

Sitting there, Thalasia stared at the stage and half-listened to the mermaid that had taken the spotlight. Her voice was okay. Better than the prior option. She could go up there. She even knew what song she'd sing. But all eyes would be on her. It was different when she handled creatures one on one or went into defense mode.

Setting one glass of clear liquid in front of her with an audible thud, Aurelia narrowed her eyes. "Well? Decided yet? Or should I just torch the place?"

"You realize the risk that goes with it?" She lifted the glass to her lips and took a sip. Thalasia frowned. "I thought you were getting us drinks."

Aurelia gave her a confused tilt of her head before taking a swig herself. "What the fuck is this shit? Water?" She turned and faced the bar in a fury.

The barkeep stood one table over with a tray of shot glasses in her hand.

"Hey barkeep! I ordered drinks, not water," Aurelia hollered.

Coming over to their table, the barkeep snickered. "No need to get violent. Every newcomer gets Safe Juice until I decide if you're gonna cause trouble in my bar."

Thalasia raised a hand and pushed the glass of water aside. "We're not here to cause problems."

"Then tell me what you're here for." The barkeeper set the tray of drinks on their table.

She stole a quick glance at Aurelia. How much did they reveal? Other species may have seen the broken barrier by now. Thalasia interlaced her fingers together. "Information. You got any of that? If not, leave the drinks and we'll be good."

"Lucky for you, I'm the best source of information in this bar. I'd say town, but sometimes the fae know things I don't." Her lips curled at the corners. "Tell ya what. I'll make you ladies a deal."

Aurelia's hand constricted around the glass of water until it fractured in her grip. "Your *deal* best involve answers... and a way to those fae," the dragon grumbled.

"In case you haven't noticed, there's a bunch of them in here. But I've heard most of their tales. As for answers... yeah, sure. You just have to get songbird here on stage." Bearing a wide grin, she set a shot glass of black liquid in front of each of them. "Cheers, ladies." The last shot she lifted in the air, knocked it back, and returned to the bar, empty tray in hand.

Hanging her head, Thalasia rubbed her temples with a groan. Whose brilliant idea had this been again? Oh, right? Hers. She was the idiot with all the bright ideas. Maybe she just needed to stop having them.

"I'm not drinking that." Aurelia pointed at the black drink, brushing the shard of glass from her palm. "I don't trust these people. If you've got concerns I should know about before we proceed, now's the time. She's clearly fucking with us. What's you getting on stage give her?"

"She's a half-breed. Of course she's fucking with us, but that doesn't mean she doesn't get something out of the deal. It could be..." Her words trailed off as a satyr came up to the table with several plates of food. He set out platters of lizard kabobs, fish fillets, moth-rings, and fried plums. Thalasia waited until he left before speaking again. "... several things. Mutual information, that we're down here, more control over the crowd... there's a long-standing history between half-breeds and full-breeds, but that doesn't mean I know how it would impact us."

Eyeing the shot, she picked up one of the fried plums and took a bite.

Aurelia thrust a hand through her golden waves in frustration. She turned to face the stage, eyes reassessing the rowdy crowd. Surveying the room, she conducted a headcount of potential fae.

Screw it. Things couldn't get worse. Not after what happened in the store. Thalasia wrapped her hand around the shot glass and tossed the black liquid back. It was sweet, yet it still burned down the back of her throat. For a moment, she even felt a little lighter, almost as if she was soaring through the sky with the sun at her back. A small smile made its way across her lips as she took another bite of the plum. "You were the one telling me to get up there. What if her challenge is just to keep me off the stage?"

Aurelia offered a suspicious glance at her. "And what if it's specifically to get you up there and expose your power—or something you don't know you have? Like that *catalyst.*" She held up a hand before Thalasia could protest. "I know you said you had no such thing. Whatever. Say I believe you. If we're wrong and you expose that kind of artifact to another, who's saying they won't add to our growing list of problems and enemies? My guards can hold the barrier, but I'm not looking to reignite a war between the earthbound and the dragons."

Swallowing the last bite of plum, Thalasia leaned forward on the agate table and picked up a lizard kabob. She wasn't positive her so-called artifact had anything to do with opening the bridge, but she definitely didn't plan on taking any chances with someone getting their hands on it. Her gaze flicked to the stage. She could get up there, and belt out a single song without touching a quarter of her power, even with a crowd this size. "I'm able to control my power. And if I *had* an artifact of any kind, don't you think I would've been smart enough to hide it with the way Enoch kept eyeing the hell out of me? Or do you really think I'm *that* stupid?"

Aurelia grinned. "I think you just admitted to hiding *something.* But seeing as you're a notch above this lot, I'm willing to let it go a little longer. That said, I noticed the prisoner eyeing your shiny neck charm. He's been a recluse since the war with very few visitors—beside my predecessor and myself. He's a far cry from stupid, but he's a bit out of practice with social cues. And seeing as he's... him, I doubt he was staring at your rack. His unspoken interest in your necklace didn't escape me—nor its sudden lack of weight since then."

With a sigh, Aurelia spotted her target at a table in the corner of the room. "What if the stage isn't what it seems? What if it's spelled? Not unlike the skinchanger's store. The half-breeds have a natural advantage here. Even if you think you're being clever, we shouldn't underestimate them. The first rule of war is to never underestimate your opponent. Desperation can push anyone to their limits and beyond. Envision the worst and assume that's the outcome."

Aurelia resigned, pushing off the table to make her way toward the fairy hiding in the corner. "You and Seru are better versed in siren tricks and half-breeds. Just don't overplay your hand, Thalasia. I've no choice but to save you, if you do. But setbacks aren't in our best interest here. Announcing to the world that a full-blooded siren and dragon have come down to play isn't going to set anyone's mind at ease."

"You think I've been sitting here staring at the stage for my health? Obviously, it's imbued with magic, but I don't think it's as bad as we're thinking." Thalasia glanced from the jockey to the barkeep, paying attention to the looks they kept giving one another and them. "Of course, we could be completely overthinking this. But you go do what you're gonna do and I'll happily sit here and eat." She ripped a hunk of leg from the lizard on the kabob stick.

Aurelia sashayed her way to a table near the fairy, helping herself to a seat with a less obvious pair—a fox and a fire spirit of some sort.

Thalasia snagged the shot that she'd left behind and drank it in one swallow, then continued to munch on the food at the table. It had been hours since she'd eaten. She glanced across the room at Aurelia. She didn't appear to be having much luck with the two women she'd sat with. Rolling her eyes, Thalasia bit off another hunk of lizard.

The dragon-girl still thought for sure her charm had been responsible for opening the barrier. She couldn't dispute it, but she couldn't confirm it either. Her gaze flitted to the stage as one of the half-breed sirens they'd seen earlier took it. Thalasia narrowed her eyes and stared.

The half-breed had selected something upbeat and fun. She moved in sync to the music, her voice much better than the mermaid. Still nothing compared to her own. Not to mention, there was no power behind the attempted vocal range. And a slight lack of control. Thalasia grinned. She could sing this half-siren under the sky and back again.

Why had she pushed so hard against this? If she'd been by herself, she would've found the perfect moment, like now, and gotten up there to charm the crowd without question. But she wasn't by herself. And over the last few days, her emotions had gone unchecked. Her time with Seru had reacquainted her with holes in her heart she'd forgotten about over the years.

Despite that, she was still a siren. One who could charm the hell out of these creatures. And it was high-time she acted like it. Her mother raised her better than this. Thalasia glanced back at Aurelia. Just maybe it would help the dragon-shifter out.

Setting her food aside, Thalasia stood and made her way through the crowd. When she got to the box where the KJ worked, she ascended the short flight of stairs and whispered her song selection to the woman.

The karaoke jockey smiled. "Good choice."

Of course it was. When she'd decided on a song earlier, only one came to mind—"Carry Me" by Eurielle. It was something she'd come across in one of her many times around a human town. She suspected a lot of that music had gotten heard on Prisma Isle too, although maybe not all of it. Nor did she know how. She hadn't seen one human, that she recalled.

Thalasia climbed onto the blue stone slab and took her place center stage. As the soft orchestral began, she thought once more of Seru and opened her mouth. She vocalized the first verse low and deep, allowing her voice to transition naturally through the words, her aria easily heard above the music.

The entire bar fell into a mellow silence as the power behind the tune hit their ears. Every set of eyes turned and faced her. The ache of her loneliness came across as she sang to her love, telling him she'd keep their memories close until they could be together once again.

Belting out the chorus of the song, the melody of her voice lifted as if hope carried her across the sky to where her love awaited her. She thought back to her parents and how they cherished one another. It had been a sight to see them dance by the fire, tenderly serenading each other without a care in the world. The day they were killed left her empty, a shell of who she could have been.

Whether he meant to, Seru mended some holes in her heart with his kindness, the way he protected her, and how he continuously reached out even when she tried to push him away. A single tear rolled down her cheek as she continued into the second verse. He was the light in a dark world that had swallowed her years ago.

Her hands danced across the air as she weaved the notes together with her movements. Each perfectly harmonized word sent a deep-rooted sense of peace and willingness to please through the hushed crowd. The lyrics of the chorus left her mouth again. She noted the ongoing scene between Aurelia and a leprechaun, but didn't pay it too much mind. If she did, she'd risk losing control of her charm with a crowd this size.

The gentle trill of her voice carried around the bar as her gaze met each individual pair of eyes. Thalasia connected temporarily with the soul of every creature there, as though she serenaded them alone. It was the best way to ensure they remembered nothing but her song. Her silver eyes sparkled as she concluded the last chorus, her fingers caressing the air as if she had become whole because she and her love had found their way home to each other.

As she hummed along with the last of the orchestral music, she thought of Seru and her face shined for a moment. She didn't know if any of the tranquility had made its way to him, but she hoped it had.

The song ended. Before the mass of creatures erupted in applause, Thalasia stepped down from the stage and headed back to her and Aurelia's corner table. She glanced around the bar and sat up straighter. Where was Aurelia? She didn't see her anywhere.

The barkeep came over and set another shot of the black liquid on the table. "Looking for your friend?"

"Yes."

"She left a couple of minutes ago, which is a good thing, since she can't seem to keep her power in check. Tell her next time to leave it at the door or she isn't welcome back."

Thalasia frowned. She left her alone for all of five minutes. Had the scene gotten that out of hand? Drawn that much attention? "Noted. Now, how about you share the information you promised?"

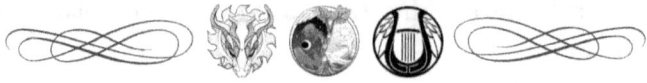

"Open up, it's me."

The door to Seru's room swept inward, an unseen wind welcoming the siren inside. Seru sat at the edge of the bed, huddled in a blanket. His dark hair was a tousled mess, but his gray eyes appeared refreshed and clear. He greeted Thalasia with a sheepish smile and nod.

Aurelia leaned forward from where she'd been holding up the far wall. In an instant, she seized the opportunity proffered by his distraction to snatch the object from his grasp.

Stepping inside, Thalasia offered a small nod back to Seru. She closed the door behind her and tossed the cloak on the opposite bed. "What was that?"

"A prize."—Seru drew out the word, inciting a snort from Aurelia—"the matriarch lifted from the friend she made at the bar." The barest hints of amusement tinted his tone. "I hope your quest fared better."

Shaking her head, Thalasia stepped further into the room and cringed. "Aside from Aurelia's scene, yes, I got the information promised."

Aurelia turned the thing over in her hands, inspecting every crevice in the flickering candle light. The long wooden object's smooth surface contained several carved intricacies. Painstakingly beautiful craftsmanship. Despite that, nothing more than a pipe.

"It appears the leprechaun smokes." The corner of Seru's mouth twitched as he beheld Aurelia's continued inspection of the simple, everyday object.

She cast him a nasty glare, her lips unfurling to reveal her pointed fangs. "Who conceals a pipe?" Aurelia asked him, not for the first time.

Seru returned to a more neutral demeanor before rising to his feet, albeit unsteadily. Both women shot him concerned glances. He waved them off, securing the blanket around his shoulders to conceal his still-bare chest. "An old man seeking relief from his maladies, perhaps?"

Thalasia groaned and dragged a hand through her blue locks. She tugged at the hem of the too-short blue dress. "You stole that from the leprechaun. Great, just great."

Noting Thalasia's sudden discomfort, Seru offered her the blanket and averted his gaze, hoping to keep Aurelia's commentary to a minimum. He had little doubt who'd selected the night's attire.

"He had his grubby mitts all over my dress, so don't go feeling too sorry for him. I even paid that frigid wench manning the bar while leaving that ridiculous establishment fully intact. I call that generous."

Hesitantly, Thalasia sought the comfort Seru offered.

"Yes," Seru turned toward Aurelia, his words dripping with sarcasm, "Generous is by far the most apt choice for exposing your powers while simultaneously agitating the townspeople, whom—in case you've forgotten—we need on our side."

"And what did you find in that glorious black abyss behind your eyelids while we were gone?" Aurelia challenged. "Nothing, that's what!"

Seru offered a weary sigh in response. He rested his head in his hand, shaking it in disbelief. Would she ever learn?

"Yeah, well, the barkeep made it clear if you can't keep your powers in check, we aren't welcome back." Thalasia smirked.

Aurelia turned to Thalasia, her fists finding her hips. "My powers were *in check*. Besides, who *wants* to go back to that trash heap, anyway?"

Holding out a hand to Thalasia, Seru sighed. "Perhaps we should take our leave. Allow the matriarch to cool her temper."

Thalasia opened her mouth and snapped it shut. Sliding her hand in Seru's, she nodded. "Yeah. Tomorrow is going to be another long day."

Seru poked his head out to check that the hall was empty before quietly escorting Thalasia to her room. Aurelia continued her rant in the background, her back to the pair as they made their escape. He allowed Thalasia to enter first, sure to secure the door behind them. He kept his back to her as he spoke. "I'm sorry for your unfortunate selection of... attire for the evening. Aurelia doesn't understand that other species are more self-conscious or select different garments out of modesty. If you wish to change into something more comfortable, I'll gladly keep my back turned while you..."

He leaned his forehead against the wooden slab. Words shouldn't be this hard. They never had been before. *Why am I suddenly feeling so self-conscious? She probably thinks my concern for her clothing in the face of more pressing issues is utterly ridiculous.*

"Yes, thank you." There was a soft rustling sound as clothes got replaced. "You can turn around now."

"You're welcome." His eyes immediately shifted from her face to the tank top to the makeshift skirt. "I think you may have uncovered the latest fashion trend, besides proving yourself a master sleuth." He pushed away from the door to claim a seat on the bare mattress.

Her cheeks flushed with a small chuckle. She strode over and sat next to him. "As long as I don't trip, I might be the model of the century."

"You're an absolute vision," Seru responded. "No matter what you wear. It's what's inside that makes the woman, not the clothes she wears—or even the identities she takes on."

"Thank you." A small smile settled on her lips. "And I wouldn't discount Aurelia entirely. She played right into the half-breed's hands and pushed me into a challenge I couldn't refuse."

He shook his head at Aurelia's predictable nature, though he was glad the pair had worked together effectively enough to get information. "Pushy and demanding are her strengths. She plays them well. However, I hope she didn't cause you too much trouble with her little... outburst."

Thalasia's fingers tightened their grasp on the blanket as her neck flushed with heat. She blinked. It subsided as quickly as it had appeared. "Um ... no. After she left, my charm calmed most of the crowd. And the half-breed settled the leprechaun. Then came to me as promised."

Seru gave her his full attention, watching curiously as she reacted. His expression fell. "I'm sorry if what happened on the docks earlier made you uncomfortable," he offered. "I was afraid what little grip remained would slip. And I didn't want to hurt you. Didn't want to allow my beast to..."

Words failing him seemed to be the night's theme. But he felt obligated to give her something. He certainly couldn't take back his earlier behavior resulting from their encounter with the skinchanger. It made sense for Thalasia to feel uncomfortable and afraid. His beast inspired nothing but fear. He felt silly straying from their objective to offer such a feeble attempt at reconciliation instead of maintaining a keen focus and allowing her to divulge her newly discovered clues.

She reached out and grasped his arm. "It isn't your fault. I blame myself. We could've gone somewhere else... or we could've left when you first felt off. I didn't help with any of that. And then after..." Thalasia sighed. "I hated seeing you like that and not being able to help."

Resting his hand on hers, Seru gave it a firm squeeze. "Please, don't blame yourself, Thalasia. No one—and I mean no one, myself included—can predict how and when my beast is going to rear its ugly head. The degradation of the magic binding the collar doesn't aid in that. It makes me even more dangerous to be around. You came out of concern, not to make things worse. You were brave."

He offered her the best smile he could muster. "There's little you could have done to soothe me in that moment. The skinchanger and his unexpected prowess caught us both off guard. I'm just thankful you didn't take off afterward. I can't imagine how upset and frightened you must have been after all that."

Readjusting on the bed, she turned to him, tilted her head, and cupped his cheek. "I wasn't scared. Not of you. I could never..."

Her sentiment touched him. The smile faltered, replaced by more of a grimace as he took her hands in his. How could he explain? "My beast is me... a part of me. But it's also... not me," he tried, struggling to articulate his turmoil. "Under normal circumstances, you have nothing to fear of me. But when the beast rises, I'm not sure I'm much more than a spectator to its actions. I have no control or influence. I can't stop it. And that's what I want you to fear."

As he continued, his grip tightened and his voice became more beseeching. "If you ever lose me to it, I want you to be afraid. I want you to flee and get as far away from me as you can."

She stared at him in disbelief. Her eyebrows knitted together as tears prickled the corners of her silver eyes. "I can't promise you that. I can't promise I won't do everything in my power to help. To bring you back, to make you whole—"

"I cherish your pure heart and desire to help Thalasia. I do, truly. But what happens when you can't bring me back once I'm lost?"

"I can't think like that."

"I don't want to see you injured or killed," he pleaded.

Thalasia stood, clutching the blanket around her waist as she paced the room. After a minute, she stopped, kneeled down in front of him, and lifted her eyes to his. "A few days ago, you asked me to consider the idea of a future. To reconsider my plans. I have, but if you're not in them, then nothing else matters. Whether I have you as a friend, or this becomes more... if I lost you, then I'm lost, too."

Seru startled at her admission, eyes wide and mouth agape. He blinked a few times, unsure of what to say. He cleared his throat to buy himself some time. "Thalasia, I... You think too much of me. You deserve so much better than what my twisted existence could ever give you. I'm as likely to eat you as I am to—"

A strong pounding came at the door. "Seru! I don't know what you two snuck off to conspire about this time, but—"

Seru jumped to his feet and yanked open the door, pulling Aurelia inside before she could wake the entire inn. She allowed herself to be escorted in, his vice grip on her arm readying her for a second argument. Her words caught in her throat as she noticed Thalasia. "Why is she half naked?" she demanded, her nose wrinkled in disgust.

He blew out a breath he hadn't realized he'd been holding, raking a hand through his mane as he paced the short distance between Aurelia and the bed.

Before either spoke, Aurelia cut in. "If her newfound secrets involve anything hidden under that blanket, you two are officially on your own."

Thalasia's shoulders slumped. She swallowed and got to her feet. Wrapping her arms around herself, she sat on the edge of the bed and dropped her eyes to the floor. "There's a trail just outside of town, Crow Skull Trail. It isn't a road like what we used to get into the market, but she said we'd know it. We'll take that to Diminutive Beach, where we'll find Chicane Village. There's a green-winged siren there who knows about the bridge... and the prophecy. It'll take us most of the day to get there."

"Crow Skull. I like the sounds of that." Aurelia grinned.

Seru frowned, allowing his limbs to drop, deflated. "Green-winged siren..." he attempted to process, despite his churning emotions. "I thought you said there weren't any others with feathers as vibrant as yours?"

"Seru! I'm sorry you didn't get laid, but stop dropping the pressure in the room." Aurelia rubbed her bare arms. "You're creating a draft."

His face flushed a fiery crimson. "Aurelia, not every opportunity yields sex. We were just talking!" he thundered. His hand flew to his mouth. He hadn't meant to shout.

Aurelia gave him a surprised raise of her brow, but nothing more. She pursed her lips, unable to stop herself. "I thought jealousy was *his* color, not yours."

A bolt of lightning shot across the room and a loud crack followed by a crash. A blackened portrait, the frame splintered, and shattered glass rained to the floor.

Aurelia cringed. "Sensitive much?"

Thalasia's cheeks tinged pink as her shoulders tensed. She rested a hand at the base of her neck as her eyebrows squished together. Standing, she walked over to the window and stared out. "As far as I've known, I am the only one. I haven't exactly been around another siren in eight years. All I know is what I was taught and what I saw as a child. I didn't look anything like any of the others. Not even my parents. They were all various shades of brown. I didn't know another existed with bright colors... until I got here."

Seru did his best to quiet his heartache, turning it to anger at Aurelia's petty provocations did little good.

"We aren't as fond of rainbows as you might think," Aurelia said, crossing her arms and pointing her nose in the air.

"Sirens aren't either," Thalasia replied.

Seru strode across the room, hesitating before laying a hand softly on Thalasia's shoulder. "I'm sure whoever this green siren is must be equally afraid of being discovered." He gave her shoulder a comforting squeeze. Minuscule jolts of electricity lanced down her arms. Seru gnawed on the inside of his lip until he tasted the coppery tang of blood.

Thalasia turned and faced him. Her gaze softened as she cupped his cheek. Her touch tingled ever so gently as the skin he'd broken inside his mouth mended itself.

He offered her a tight smile, his eyes clouding with an unspoken apology. He allowed himself to lean into her touch ever so slightly.

"I'm sorry, too," Thalasia mouthed. Stroking his cheek with her thumb, she gave him a tender smile. "There are other rumors, but they're all specific to each species... nothing about the bridge. They may not yet realize it's been compromised."

Aurelia curled her finger, causing Seru to double over as she manipulated the magic in his collar. "Focus."

He stumbled but caught himself, pulling the connection taut as he resisted her pull on his invisible tether. He raised his darkening eyes to meet hers. The slight glow they gave off only furthered his irritation at her sudden change in mood. "As you command, All-Mother," he growled through bared teeth.

Aurelia's frown deepened at the response, but she received the message enough to release her hold on him. "All the better," she replied to Thalasia.

"The less they know, the better off we are. I'd rather we find a solution and seal that barrier up before they take notice."

"Or before our friends from the other side decide to try again," Seru finished for her, massaging his throat beneath the metal band as he righted himself.

Thalasia frowned. Crossing her arms, she glared at Aurelia. "Are you done? If so, then maybe we should rest for a few hours before we leave. We'll be traveling close to the fae forest, and I highly *doubt* you want them to realize you've stolen something that belongs to them. After all, you don't want to *start* a war."

"Me? You're the ones getting sidetracked!" Aurelia shot back, rolling her eyes. "You two lovebirds get some rest. I'm going for a walk." She was up and out the door before Seru could call after her. The door slammed behind her with such force the room shook.

Seru sighed heavily and settled for massaging his temples. He didn't have the energy to chase after her. "How do we always end up like this?" he asked, not really expecting an answer. "At this rate, they'll invade and rip our island apart before we puzzle out these cryptic clues."

A thought occurred to him. Aurelia hadn't taken the knapsack with her when she left, so perhaps all wasn't lost. He might still have access to his library. He moved to the door, pausing with his hand on the knob. "Goodnight, Thalasia." He smiled at her. "I have some things I'd like to look into before we resume our journey tomorrow. I'll be next door. Should you need anything at all, don't hesitate to come over."

Thalasia flashed a smile at him. "Goodnight, Seru. I'm just going to rest."

"Good choice," he said, softly bringing the door to a close behind him.

Chapter Six

The trail had been easy to recognize. Someone had staked crow skulls into the ground in front of a set of matching trees. Every mile or so, another pair of skulls met their gazes. They spent hours traveling, climbing over tree roots, and following the secret trail nearly the whole way. They hadn't seen another pair of skulls in over a mile.

Thalasia stopped. Off in the distance, she spotted a faint cloud of smoke. "We must be—"

An arrow whizzed by their heads. "The next one won't miss."

She scanned the direction the arrow and voice came from. It sounded female, although somewhat on the husky side. A good eight yards ahead, a figure occupied a tree almost thirty feet high. Thalasia narrowed her eyes and scrutinized the figure. Despite her eyesight, she couldn't make much out of the creature. They blended well with the forest. "We aren't here to cause any problems. We're looking for someone."

"Think you can knock whoever that is out of that tree, Seru?" Aurelia whispered, leaning in and bumping shoulders with him.

"I could... but I don't think that's the wisest option here. Diplomacy is better than violence."

"A sudden breeze isn't exactly violent," Aurelia said. "They shot at us first."

"We're going into someone else's territory. *You*, of all people, should understand defending it." Thalasia crossed her arms, recalling her introduction to the woman's whole fucking guard. And she wants to knock someone out because of one arrow? What was wrong with this girl?

The slight sound of leaves rustling brushed her ears. The surrounding breeze kicked up.

Whatever it was, they were moving. Thalasia attempted to follow the path the creature took as it jumped from branch to branch, but she couldn't keep up. "It can't be," she muttered. She tossed a glance over her shoulder from Seru to Aurelia and did the only thing she could think of. Removing the cloak from her shoulders, she spread her wings wide.

"I thought we weren't showing the wings!" Aurelia hissed.

Seru put himself between Aurelia and the threat. "Trust her," he said, holding Aurelia back while gauging the situation for himself.

The wind settled. "Who are you?" a deep, masculine voice asked.

Thalasia shot a quick glare to Aurelia, hoping the dragon got the hint to shut up. Shifting her attention back to the male siren she had yet to gain sight of, she straightened her spine and focused. "My name is Thalasia. These are my companions, Seru and Aurelia. We need to speak with you, please."

"Why?" His voice came from the opposite side of the forest. He'd changed places again.

That was a good question. How much of the truth did she reveal? Thalasia inhaled and exhaled a deep breath. "We were told you might have knowledge... about the bridge."

Leaves fell from a tree close by. There was a gentle creak of a branch shifting as a six-foot-tall, green-winged siren darted out from the tree line. He slowly eased to the ground, landing on the grass with the finesse of a dancer. He stood tall; a quiver full of arrows strapped across his broad chest. "What do you know about the bridge?"

"Only that it exists," Seru interceded. "That there are bizarre creatures with elemental magic on the other side."

Aurelia pushed against Seru's chest as she narrowed her eyes at the stranger. "Your turn, green bean."

"The name is Mac, dragon. Use it. *You* came to my home. Not the other way around," he spat out and crossed his arms.

For about the millionth time since this trip started, Thalasia tensed. Between the discovery of a male siren in existence and Aurelia's constant anger, she was ready to be anywhere else. "Can you please help us?"

Mac stared at the three of them, his eyes settling on Aurelia. "Ask me nicely and I'll consider answering your questions."

"I don't think—" Seru began, dismay coloring his tone.

"If I had it my way, we wouldn't be wasting time with pointless conversation," Aurelia said. "But the Regent and bluebird thought friendly was best. I got out voted."

Tapping his mouth with his finger, Mac smirked and waved them off. "I get it. You don't really need my help."

Thalasia reached a hand out. "Your village... it was attacked..." She paused and swallowed the lump in her throat. There hadn't been time to share the vision with Seru, but it was too late now. She'd already opened her mouth. "What if I heal your injured? Would you help us then?"

He stopped mid-stride and peered back at them, his emerald green eyes regarding Thalasia. "You have the touch?"

It hadn't been something she'd used on anyone in some time. Recently, she used it more on creatures, rather than people. "Yes, but I need to know beforehand. Are they different? Or like the ones across the bridge?"

"They're as unique as our colors. You have a deal." His eyes darkened as he glowered at each one of them. "But if you harm anyone in my village, I promise you death."

"Ugh..." Aurelia groaned. "Kill me now, fucking multi-colored chickens."

Seru gave her a look, urging caution, pleading for it.

Mac quickly closed the distance between himself and them. He growled, his gaze laser-focused on Aurelia. "You're welcome to leave."

"Trust me, I would, but he's grown attached to your blue doppelgänger over there." Aurelia pointed from Seru to Thalasia. "Nauseating, isn't it?"

With a snicker, Mac glimpsed at Seru and shook his head in disgust. "Fool."

"We didn't ask for your opinion." Thalasia balled up her fists. She was fucking tired of everyone throwing out their thoughts about her and Seru. Was there some problem with them caring about one another?

"And?" Mac sneered and sauntered off in the direction they'd been traveling.

Her mouth slackened, and she glared at the green-feathered freak. This was the siren she'd been given as a mission. Great, just fucking great.

Demeter had jokes. Unfurling and refolding her fists, she tucked her wings in tight and strode after the male.

Seru used his long strides to catch up with Thalasia and whispered in her ear, "You did well. You got us in. Don't allow their silly squabbling to steal your victory."

"Thank you." Without giving a shit what Mac and Aurelia thought, she laced her fingers with Seru's and gave his hand a gentle squeeze. It was the only way to squelch the fire in her belly. She was pretty certain Demeter hadn't sent her to kill the siren, no matter how much he pissed her off.

Aurelia brought up the rear, seemingly pleased to find someone who agreed with her point of view.

"What happened to your village, Mac?" Seru asked. "Beyond healing, surely there's other aid we can offer."

"We were attacked. Dark guilers sneaked in. I dropped at least two. Unfortunately, you three showed up and I haven't been able to fully assess the damage or determine what happened to the other dark guilers." Mac continued walking forward.

Dark guilers? Thalasia grimaced. "Is that how you differentiate them?"

"They have no souls." Mac snarled. "The ones I live with understand that power is a give and take relationship. For those that forget, they don't survive."

"You say they snuck in," Seru said. "Were they searching for something?"

"You think they meant to steal from them?" Aurelia asked, curiosity causing her to rejoin the conversation. "Or were they searching for some-one?"

"We aren't anywhere near the bridge." Mac glanced at the sky for a moment. "They can't maintain flight, which leaves a boat as their only way across, so yes, they snuck in. We're one of the oldest villages in Prisma Isle, either is possible."

This wasn't good. Not good at all. Thalasia's eyebrows drew together as she peered over at Seru, and then she swung her gaze forward as the tree line opened up.

Just ahead, loads of wooden huts had been sporadically built across a large shore to both the east and west. Trees of varying heights were scattered throughout the land. Some offered shade over the homes, while others bore fruit. She heard the gentle sound of crashing waves not far off in the distance. The smell of salt, acrid smoke, and sweet treats wafted through the air.

An older woman with curly paper-white hair, seven fingers on each hand, and crystal blue eyes ran up to their group. "Mac! There you are!"

"What's going on Maggie?"

Her eyes bulged out. "We've got the fires out, but I can't find Felix." Mac's gaze dropped, and he muttered something under his breath. "He was in the west end by the gardens. Did you check there?"

"Who's Felix?" Seru asked. "Give us a description. We'll help search."

"By *we*, I hope you mean *you*," Aurelia retorted, stubbornly parking herself beneath one of the fruit trees.

"I mean, all of us." Seru sounded wounded. "But if you insist on sitting this one out... Thalasia and I will gladly help." He turned to Mac and Maggie. "It may not be much," he said, touching his collar with his free hand, "but I can still fly. What do you say, Thalasia? We can split up, cover more ground from higher up."

Thalasia smiled bitterly at Aurelia's lack of involvement. Not that it should surprise her. Whatever. She was over it. She turned her attention to Seru and the situation at hand. It was a great idea. She could stretch her wings and check out the village at the same time. "Absolutely. I'd be happy to help search."

Mac cast a glance at Maggie, and then he shifted his eyes to the two of them and nodded. "Felix is the village elder; he won't be hard to miss. He's bald and his skin is covered in eggshell bumps. Just keep low. We're close to the fae forest, and they don't take kindly to strangers."

"Stay here with her," Mac said to Maggie, gesturing to Aurelia. Without another word, he shot into the sky and soared toward the west.

"Don't forget to whistle when you find him," Aurelia called after him. She paid them little mind as she rifled through her knapsack.

"Ladies first." Seru nodded to Thalasia, stepping back to give her some room.

Flashing a warm smile at him, she stretched her wings out to their full span and eased into the air as she took off for the southeast side of the village.

She could see the charcoal remains of several of the huts from above, especially those closest to the water. Although they had contained the fire, the acrid smell of smoke remained. A few of the huts had been water logged, while others had their roofs and doors ripped off. There was debris throughout the land. The damage was widespread across the village.

Felix was nowhere in the wreckage.

Mac's talons touched down on the ground where he'd left their visitors. Although he'd agreed to letting them scour part of the village, he didn't trust them. He'd executed a quick fly over the east side of the village, assessing the carnage along the way. They'd be rebuilding for months. And Felix hadn't been anywhere he'd covered. None of this would stop him from asking the visitors what they'd found. He looked from the male dragon to the siren. "Anything?"

"Nothing," Thalasia said.

Seru returned with a grim expression. He shook his head in dismay. "I found little more than ash and smoldering ruins, but no evidence of life. The guilers decimated the shore line. It appears they now have fire in their elemental arsenal. It's been a long time since I've seen destruction of this magnitude on Prisma Isle."

For crying out loud. He'd have to check with the sprites since they were always watching. Maybe they'd seen something. He eyed the sun. It was too early for that. Raising an eyebrow, Mac noticed the blonde had disappeared. Not his problem. His gaze shifted to Maggie, who sat there fidgeting. "What is it?"

"We've got a situation... in the cage."

Really? A smile tugged at the corners of his lips. He may not need the sprites after all. Directing his focus on the siren, Mac pointed at her. "Come with me."

Seru looked at Thalasia at Mac's lack of invitation.

Thalasia crossed her arms and lifted her chin in defiance. "I'm not going anywhere without Seru."

Flicking his gaze over to the male, Mac sneered. The siren might be gorgeous, but she was irritating as hell. It didn't stop the possibility that he required her help. She had abilities he didn't, and he wouldn't risk

Felix's life to spite her. Mac shifted his eyes back to her. "Fine. Bring your boyfriend."

He sauntered off toward the east side of the village and paused mid-step. It was an afterthought, but something that he should correct. Mac glanced back at Seru with a slight scowl. "For the record, they have more than fire in their arsenal. Air, fire, water, and earth."

Adding nothing more to the statement, Mac continued on expecting them to follow. He monitored them out of the corner of his eye.

Peering at the spot they'd left the blonde, Thalasia shook her head and turned to Seru. "I feel like things just went from bad to worse."

"The amount of attitude we seem to catch has certainly doubled." Seru offered her his arm. "And I can't help but wonder if the Matriarch wandering off isn't multiplying our troubles. She's clearly up to something. Let's hope Mac and his village know more about these *dark* guilers than we do. Otherwise, we're back to square one."

"You don't think she'd take advantage of us being so close to the fae, do you?" Thalasia hooked her arm in his, scrutinizing the villagers as they walked.

Seru grimaced. "It wouldn't surprise me if she's done exactly that."

Many of the villagers had returned to normal activities: collecting fire wood, tending to plants, gathering fruit and vegetables. Others were cleaning up the debris. The one thing that he expected his followers noticed about each villager was every single one of them had some deformity.

"As much as I don't want to admit it, I can see we were led here for a reason," Thalasia said.

Mac eyed Seru and Thalasia for a second, arm in arm, and frowned. Patience was not his strong suit. At least he could do something while he waited for them to catch up. He crouched down to a gaggle of guiler children and began playing air ball with them. Although each child used air magic to keep a white ball in motion, he used his wings.

Seru smiled ruefully. "I think our mighty hero and the Matriarch have much in common. They both seem to be drawn to playmates of a much younger variety."

"Great..." she drew out the word.

Sending the ball further out, Mac shooed the kids off toward the middle of the huts. He looked over at Seru and Thalasia. "Are you two done dawdling?"

She glared at him as she ground her jaw. Her grip on Seru's arm tightened. Her neck flushed, and she gritted out her response. "Just lead on."

Seru placed his hand over Thalasia's and showed a little fang as he spoke. "You shouldn't let him bait you like that. He gains satisfaction from getting under your skin, getting a rise out of you. It's how they make themselves feel more in control, more important and empowered. In reality, they're just being... well, brats."

Thalasia cracked a smile. Leaning in close, she whispered, "I guess I just hoped one part of this mission would be"—she paused as the words fell short—"easier, I guess."

Mac's eyebrows furrowed at the male's comments. Eh, he *was* the one in control. Hooking a right, he ambled to a square building that had been in the far corner of the village. It sat near the edge of the forest, completely untouched from the damage they'd seen in the rest of the huts. The place didn't have any windows or other openings.

He gave a curt nod to the young man standing post outside the door. "Anything I need to know?"

"Broken femur bone, a few gashes along the belly, possibly internal bleeding. He probably won't last long."

"Alright. Go check in with Maggie and see what she needs done." They'd have to do some reorganization for a while. They had many people and not enough homes to sleep everyone.

"Yes, sir." The young man took off past Seru and Thalasia, barely offering them a glance.

Mac crossed his arms and faced his two visitors. His eyes raked over Thalasia and the way her arm was curled around the male dragon. He couldn't stop the sneer that settled on his face at the sight of them. It really shouldn't bother him this much. Shaking the unexplained from his head, he thought about what was on the other side of the door. "You just need to heal the dark guiler inside, then leave the rest to me."

"Meaning what?" Thalasia asked.

"Maiming or killing our only lead is ill-advised," Seru cautioned. "I realize the damage done to your homes and people is severe, but allowing your emotions to cloud your judgment isn't going to bring back your friend or restore their homes and lands." He gestured to the villagers, still hard at work salvaging and rebuilding. "We may be outsiders, but Thalasia and I combined have greater experience in negotiation," Seru said with a slight wince. "And diplomacy. We also have our emotions in check. Let us try to gain this guiler's secrets without further wreckage or injury."

"My interrogation techniques work well." *But her charm is stronger than yours.* "Shut up!"

"We didn't say anything." Thalasia smirked. "But Seru's right. I'm not healing him, so you can kill him."

Frowning, Mac balled up his fists. He hadn't meant to say that aloud. The voice he'd heard hadn't been his own. He knew that much. Felix had spent too many years training him and educating him about his own kind. The man was the closest thing he had to a father. As much as he despised the idea of standing back and watching these two work together, it was the best option. He rolled his shoulders and released the tension in his back. "Fine. But if you don't find out what I need, then we do this my way."

"We can't allow that," Seru said, stepping forward. "Much like Thalasia expressed, I won't stand idly by while you terrorize or beat a man to death. Even prisoners of the lowest kind should be treated with dignity and respect."

Respect? Dignity? Mac glared at Seru as he closed the distance between them. His jaw tightened. He had no problem going toe to toe with the male. "They get what they deserve."

"We need answers, gentlemen. And this isn't going to get us to them," Thalasia said.

"With respect, neither is going in there hot-headed, ready to do violence when things don't go your way." Seru eased back.

Mac frowned. Folding to anyone else's wishes hadn't been something he'd ever done. Maybe he couldn't get a full sense of Seru's power, but he had ideas of what Thalasia should be capable of. At least if what he'd heard was true. It was something he absolutely wanted to witness. Felix was the only father he had. He looked past both of them at the sun that had yet to set. Damn. He inhaled and exhaled a deep breath. "Fine. We'll do this your way, but you both best get the answers I need. Just don't think I'm leaving the two of you in there alone."

He turned around and pushed the door open.

Thalasia placed a hand on Seru's shoulder and squeezed. "This should be fun." Her words dripped with sarcasm.

"Just be careful," he requested. "We don't yet know the limits of their power."

"I will. Besides, I don't know how effective my healing will be. I'm accustomed to animals, not people." Thalasia half-shrugged as they followed Mac.

Inside the hut was almost entirely bare. There was only a wooden table, which they had strapped the dark guiler to, tied down in four places: his chest, arms, upper and lower legs. The guiler was barely conscious. Sweat drenched his body. He had several deep, bloody gashes along his chest and abdomen. His left upper thigh was bent at an angle with a bone protruding from it.

"Looks like you've got your work cut out for you," Seru said.

Thalasia's eyes widened at the sight of the damage imposed on the creature—the broken bone protruding from a shredded thigh muscle. She gagged. Seru lifted her hand to his lips and placed a soft kiss on the back of it, allowing her to step farther into the room before letting go. She visibly swallowed and made her way to the dark guiler.

Seru stayed near the entryway, casually bringing his hand to rest on his chin and cheek—close enough to bury his nose in his sleeve. He squeezed his eyes shut for a moment and then cleared his throat before speaking a few strained words of encouragement. "You've got this, Thalasia. I'm here if you need me."

Mac stood off to the side opposite the doorway, leaning against the wall as he watched and measured every step Thalasia took. If she was truly the one from the prophecy, then this would be a sight to witness.

The table came up to her waist. She placed her hands on the dark guiler, whose eyes bulged out. "Shh. I'm here to help."

Setting one hand gently on the dark guiler's leg and the other on his arm, Thalasia hummed softly. The small room filled with the gentle aria as her hands glowed a bright silver. Slowly, the guiler's bone snapped into place, and the skin over his leg and surrounding wounds across his chest and belly mended.

Seru's jaw slackened as Thalasia worked her magic. His shoulders dropped as tension appeared to leave his body.

Mac stared as Thalasia's power radiated and healed the wounds inflicted on the dark guiler. Her song even influenced him, uncoiling the tension in his rigid body. It was her. The one his father had told him about. He'd truly thought Felix had lost his mind, telling him about prophecies that made no sense. What siren could heal? They took life; they didn't give it.

Her existence should frighten him, but it didn't. He wanted to know what else she was capable of. How far did her powers extend?

Thalasia's shoulders sagged as she continued to heal the unseen damage. The wounds ran deep. As the last of the injuries closed, her song ended, and she stumbled backwards, nearly tripping over her own two feet.

Mac shot upright, but didn't move from his spot against the wall. For a split second, he considered it. And that bothered him. He didn't touch people, and they didn't touch him. Felix was the one exception, and it had taken years to garner that trust. His desire to reach out and physically aid anyone, especially a woman, disturbed him.

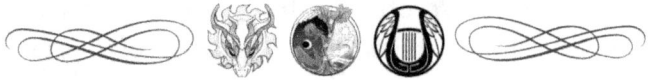

Her stomach did somersaults. Bile threatened to come up the back of her throat. Good Demeter, she was going to throw up.

"Easy." Seru closed the space between them, offering support to help steady her. His nose wrinkled up. "We should give her a moment to rest. It'll take the guiler time to recover and regain consciousness."

Mac nodded. He still hadn't left his spot on the wall. "Yeah."

"You did it." Seru sang her praise, nuzzling his cheek into hers as he carried her away from the creature on the table.

Leaning heavily on Seru, she half-covered her mouth and muttered, "Take me outside, please."

Seru easily took her weight and escorted her back out in to the open air, where the not-so-refreshing stench of smoke greeted them. Still, it was easier to breathe than the foulness in the guiler's hut.

"I can take you above the clouds if you like? Away from the smog to cleaner air," Seru offered, his arm hugging her to him. "Anything you need, just name it."

Animals were so much easier than people. Getting away from the horrid smell sounded like pure bliss. At least her stomach began settling. "Yes. That would be great. It took more out of me than I thought it would."

Without a moment's hesitation, Seru cloaked them in clouds and took to the skies. He remained steady and gentle. Once they hit the veritable clouds, it went momentarily dark before they broke through high above.

The sprawling fluff illuminated by the vibrant hues of dusk reflected off their surface. Pinks, oranges, blues, and purples.

The air was thin, but clean. Much easier to breathe than the ground-level toxins. "Promise not to run screaming," he whispered jovially. He hugged her close.

Run screaming? She chuckled at the humor. She wasn't going to run anywhere for a bit.

Above the clouds, unseen by anyone below, Seru truly transformed. His beast stretched, its serpentine form reflecting those same marvelous colors glistened in the sun. The massive creature rumbled a contented sigh. The saint beast hovered on top of the clouds, weaving with her perched atop its shimmering back.

Clutching her hands into his thick mane, Thalasia drank in as much as she could see of Seru's form. He was absolutely stunning. The color of his scales consistently changing to match the varying hues of the sky and clouds. She beamed, biting her bottom lip as she remained mindful of her talons. Briefly, she considered revealing the truth, but decided best against it. Instead, she curled her talons away from his skin. With the air rushing at her face, she stroked his shoulder, enjoying the leathery feel beneath her fingers.

Seru kept her aloft until the sun vanished beneath the clouds, leaving a stunning star-scape to fill its absence.

Thalasia gasped as she watched the sun dip below the clouds and disappear. The glow of the moon and the shine of the stars taking its place. It was absolutely serene. She'd seen nothing like this before. Watching the sky change from this height, sitting atop Seru's back—it was an experience she'd forever treasure.

The night sapped warmth quicker at this altitude. The drop in temperature didn't bother her... much. Goosebumps crawled up her arms, but she didn't care—she wouldn't change the two of them being up here together. She wanted to hold on as long as they could—away from the judgment, the snarky remarks, the dismissive looks... if she could, she'd stay up here with Seru forever.

He bobbed, testing her grip before diving back into the clouds. She couldn't communicate with him in this form, at least not verbally. Thalasia sifted her fingers through his mane and curled her arms around his wide neck, hugging him as best she could, hopeful he understood exactly what she was saying.

Halfway down, Seru shed his scales. The beast burrowed into its dark, quiet hiding place as he reclaimed his human skin. He wrapped his arms around her as they freefell back toward the earth. "Feeling better?" he shouted over the whipping winds. The widest smile she'd ever seen graced his mouth.

"Much, much better," she hollered back, lighting up as she partially unfurled her wings to slow their descent. She just wanted to prolong their time together a little longer. It was nice to see him so happy. That's exactly how it felt, down to her bones. And she prayed to Demeter she got to see it again and again.

By the time they reached the surface, the life the world above had breathed into them was swallowed by the grim reality they returned to. Near the center of the village, in the largest clearing, was a bonfire that still burned. Several young guilers gathered around, sharing food that they'd collected for dinner. West of the fire, all the children had simple cotton linens laid out to sleep on. There had to be forty to fifty in varying ages. They had been arranged in a circle with the older children on the outside.

They had laid the linens for the adults between the children and the forest's edge. Some were already curled up and resting, while a few couples snuggled close together. Mac and Maggie stood off to the side of the bonfire, speaking in hushed tones.

Seru gripped Thalasia's hand. "They've been through enough. Perhaps we should see to the formerly wounded on our own?"

She could see the weight placed on the group. So many lives torn asunder by one wrong move. Thalasia bit the inside of her cheek, squeezed his hand, and swallowed. She had to tell him of her suspicion. First, they needed to deal with the *dark* guiler. "I agree."

Seru led the way back to the hut, scanning the area along the way. His eyebrows drew together. He halted their progress just out of sight of the guard stationed in front of the hut. They huddled behind a fallen tree, charred black like the rest of the area. He shook the concern from his face. "Any chance you could charm the guard? If not, I could cause a distraction, but... calling up a lightning storm feels extreme."

She could see he was worried about Aurelia, who hadn't yet returned. She hadn't dealt with the fae before. Even the ones in the bar she'd avoided.

But she'd witnessed bits and pieces of the dragon-shifter's power. She should be able to take care of herself. Or so she hoped.

Thalasia grinned at Seru's suggestion. "Yes, I can. And it would definitely draw less attention."

Instead of singing, she simply whistled. It sounded like nothing more than the gentle chirping of a bird carried across the wind. The guard swayed to the noise as he slowly slumped to the ground. "That work?"

Seru awarded her with a radiant smile. "Always so full of surprises, aren't you?"

"I'm not the only one." She bit her bottom lip. Cracking a grin, she led him toward the square building.

When they slipped inside, Thalasia gasped. The guiler was still tied down and fully alert. The difference—someone had cleaned up all the blood. Only a faint metallic smell lingered, covered by lavender and water.

Seru turned to behold the guiler. "Hello. We'd like to speak to you about what happened here. Would you be willing to speak to us? We aren't from this village and harbor no ill will. We merely seek to understand what it is you hope to accomplish here."

It wasn't entirely true. Hopefully, Seru's statements portrayed a sense of neutrality. Regardless, the door was open if the man wished to speak.

The guiler hissed. "No talk. Nothing to say."

"My,"—Seru faltered for a moment—"friend, here,"—He swept a hand toward Thalasia in a grand gesture—"healed your wounds. Would you mind if she performed a quick once-over to ensure everything is mended?"

Thalasia tried to act like she didn't notice how Seru stumbled over his words. Not that she would've done any better, despite the word Mac used to describe Seru earlier. She shook the thought from her head and offered a kind smile to the guiler. "That's okay. If you'll allow me..."

The guiler narrowed his black, beady eyes and glanced between Seru and Thalasia. After a moment, he nodded.

She started with the torn pants leg where his thigh had been mangled. Eyeing the healed skin, Thalasia began humming. She combined her charm and soothing touch to relax the guiler. Moving up to the wounds that had been along his belly, she continued her work to lull him into submission.

Seru watched her work her magic, careful to keep an eye trained on the guiler for any suspicious activity or attempts at an escape.

She didn't know enough about what the guilers could do, so she stayed away from his face. Inspecting the new skin, she hummed a little longer and noticed his body had gone lax and his eyes had glossed over. Her eyebrows knitted together as the corners of her lips tugged into a small smile. "Your wounds look good. How did you get them?"

The guiler bobbed his head side to side. "I fought one of the guilers here. They aren't like us."

Thalasia glanced over her shoulder at Seru and winked. "I think we're ready."

Chapter Seven

S eru nodded, stepping forward. "Let's try again. Who are you? Why
have you come to Prisma Isle?"

The guiler smiled. "We are the rogue. We needed the one with the
answers."

"Who is 'the one?'" Thalasia asked. She had her suspicions, but didn't
want to assume she knew the answer. It was good to confirm, though, in
case she was wrong.

"He is the oldest among us."

"Felix," Seru confirmed. "What answers do you seek?"

The guiler struggled against his bindings. "His knowledge is great."

Thalasia frowned. He shouldn't be moving like that. Was her charm
wearing off? She placed a hand on the guiler's leg and gasped. His skin was
hot to the touch. "He's burning up."

"If he's our fire starter, that could be a problem." Seru called up a tiny
storm cloud over the guiler and a gentle rain showered down on the guiler.

The guiler hissed and snarled at the water, cooling him.

Raising an eyebrow, Thalasia canted her head. "I'm going with yes."

"We will come. You cannot stop us," the guiler said.

"He's adapting to and overcoming your charm at a startling rate. If this
continues, he's going to break free and cause a scene, drawing the villagers
and their guardian to us." Seru hopped on the table, pinning the guiler
and securing his wrists. Even if she couldn't calm the creature, at least Seru

could ensure the male stayed put. Fire—no matter how hot—wouldn't burn him.

"Can you calm him?" Seru asked. "I know you've used a lot of your power already. Don't overdo it."

Thalasia nodded. She'd need to do a good replenish soon, but she could do this. She walked over and positioned herself at the head of the guiler. Inhaling a deep breath, she pressed her hands against his shoulders. She exhaled a gentle but strong aria, her whole body lighting an iridescent silver.

The guiler slowly settled, but it didn't stop him from trying to fight their combined force off.

Catching the resonance of her silvery aura helped settle Seru. He looked at Thalasia. "I think we're going to need a boat."

"We'll be better off flying. We'll need to stay out of sight. They have arrows." She winced a little as she removed her hands from the guiler's shoulders. She remembered the ache of the hole in her wing, which also reminded her of the charm she'd buried in there.

"I remember your wounds from the time we met," Seru recalled. "It seems to have healed well. A few darker feathers as a memento. Do you still feel it?"

She sighed. Maybe now was the right time, just not in front of the guiler. If she could, they'd sneak off somewhere to really discuss this. She suspected he would have questions. "We should talk about that."

Seru slid off the table once the guiler settled. He raised a brow at her remark and followed her out into the open. The salty breeze churned up the ash, wisps swirling around their ankles. It played with his windblown mane. He did his best to tame the unruly hair, tickling his face and obscuring his view.

They walked off a way, stopping beneath a small grove of fruit trees, a quiet little alcove removed from the village of guilers and Mac.

Thalasia opened her mouth and snapped it shut. She tried again, but couldn't get the words to come out. Maybe she needed to try this a different way. She extended her left wing and took his hand in her own. When she ran his hand over her feathers and along the skin beneath them, she shivered at the touch.

Seru knitted his brows together. His fingers gently explored the bizarre texture of the skin beneath her feathers. "What... is that?" The skin was soft with a touch of a scar tissue along the edge. An object shifted beneath the surface, undefinable on its own.

She fidgeted, wringing her fingers. "It's a charm my mother gave me before she died. In the shape of a lyre. I used to wear it around my neck." Thalasia swallowed as she touched the base of her throat. This was the last thing she wanted to think about, but she couldn't stop now that she'd started. "The last thing she told me was to protect it at all costs. Nothing else was ever mentioned about it. I didn't know it was anything more than a bobble, a memory, until I saw two of its strings had snapped."

His gaze shifted as he withdrew his hand. "A lyre... like the engraving on the blue slats of the bridge!" His eyes lit up. "The colors are like a rainbow... red, orange, yellow, green, blue, violet, and purple." His expression thoughtful, he bounced on the balls of his feet. "If the engravings match your charm, they're definitely connected. A lyre is a siren's instrument. The other symbols... what if they belong to other species on Prisma Isle? There was also a draconic visage encircled by a sun," he continued, monologuing as Thalasia looked on. "Aurelia derives her power from her connection with the sun and stars. Historically, the Matriarch—" He forcefully dug his fangs into his lips, halting before he completed his sentence. His eyebrows squeezed together.

"Yes, like the one on the bridge. I recognized it when I saw the symbol that day. I know it's a representation of sirens. It's possible the others are connected to the other species here." But she had no clue what it all meant. She considered what little he'd stated about Aurelia's powers. She understood his hesitation. There was little she knew about her own people's history. Well, the sirens' history. Or at least a lot of conflicting information. "We all get our power from somewhere. I get mine from the moon." She swallowed. None of this had been her reason for showing him what she'd hidden. Thalasia scanned their surroundings, grateful night had fallen. She trusted Seru. No one else needed to know what they were discussing. "The charm has been passed through my family for centuries. Aurelia... Enoch... they may be right. Even if it was unintentional, I may be the one responsible for the barrier. My people's history... I've never been able to make sense of it."

"You're all special," he said, bringing his fingers to his lips. "My access to siren history is limited. I'd wager if we gained access to your people's history, we'd find a similar connection. Unfortunately, our people haven't always seen eye to eye," he lamented. "So, even if we were to gain permission via a diplomatic envoy to visit Pteryrina, there's no guarantee we could persuade the sirens to grant us access to their records—their accurate records." He turned to Thalasia, clearly conflicted. "There are things... knowledge I possess. Knowledge I *shouldn't* possess, that I can't share with you... from before the War..." Seru trailed, searching for a better way to express what he knew, but couldn't say. He dug his talons into his arms in frustration. "These dark guilers from Candescent Isle, I think they're seeking information from our histories. Our *shared* histories. From a time before the barrier was erected. That's why they kidnapped the village elder, Felix," Seru murmured. "Could he be old enough to have lived during those times?"

Thalasia closed her eyes. And they had come full circle. Whatever was in their histories... the barrier... that's why they'd been led here. From the beginning. Whatever had been broken... it was time to fix it. She lifted her gaze to Seru. "Mac would know. I suspect he knows more than what we've been told. It would explain my visions of him." She paused and bit her bottom lip. "He isn't the only one I'm supposed to find. The other female, a manticore, I think."

"As much as I hate to admit it," Seru said, his expression souring. "I think you're right. It's time we collect Aurelia and reconvene with that unfriendly siren and the guilers of this village. Perhaps we can somehow convince the two troublemakers to investigate other species while we find your manticore—a less than friendly bunch—and pay a visit to the sirens? I'm not sure how much more of their combined arrogance I can tolerate. One is bad enough, but two..."

Thalasia chuckled. He had a valid point. If she preferred anyone's company, it would be his over those two. She'd been perturbed enough to last a lifetime. "I'd be more than happy to shove Mac onto Aurelia. They seem made for each other."

Seru laughed, shaking his head. "I don't know. She might roast and eat him. But I think that's a chance I might take."

She crossed her arms and tapped her chin. "I just don't know how I can..." she stopped. Maybe she didn't have to sneak into Pteryrina or slip Seru in either. That half-breed might have proven more useful than she thought. "The barkeep told me there's rumor of a siren being seen around the edges of the forest. Maybe we just need to find her."

He sobered a bit as they made their way back toward the bonfire. "Was there anything in your... visions, something that could help point us toward the right manticore? I presume she's not going to be as obvious as Mac in coloration."

She shook her head at Seru's humor. She didn't care about Mac's attitude, but he was the last male siren. Hmm, then again, she didn't know that for sure. "They're only small glimpses, but I think she was traveling. I'll recognize her, though."

Seru reached out for her hand as they walked. "One obstacle at a time, I suppose."

She didn't even think about it as she laced her fingers with his. It had become so natural between them. "Quite true."

As they entered the circle, few remained awake save Mac, who sat on a log, alone, staring into the fire. Seru faced her. "I think I'll turn this one over to you. He doesn't seem terribly fond of me."

Thalasia narrowed her eyes. Yeah, she might get further by herself. "Okay. I don't think I'll be long. I'm gonna find some food after. Then maybe we can locate Aurelia?"

He nodded. "If she hasn't returned on her own by then, yes."

"I'll keep my fingers crossed." She squeezed his hand. "Wish me luck."

Leaning in, Seru kissed her cheek. "I wish you all the luck in the world," he whispered, casting one last look at Mac before shaking his head and going his own way.

Beaming, she watched him walk off for a moment, and then she turned toward the fire.

"You and lover boy finally finish?" Mac asked upon her approach.

Don't kill him. Without asking, she sat on a nearby log. Demeter had a sense of humor. She'd never stop believing that. "We got what we could out of the guiler, if that's what you're referring to. They came here specifically for Felix. The question is why?"

"He's the oldest guiler, over three-hundred-*solaris*. He knows everything there is to know about guilers. I need to get him back," he replied nonchalantly.

Solaris? Not a word she'd heard before. Though she assumed it had something to do with the male's age. Something she didn't question. Because they needed to get the guy back. Except the prisoner didn't say where they'd taken Felix. She and Seru had their suspicions, but they hadn't confirmed it. "We think they took him to Candescent Isle."

"I think so too. I just need to figure out a plan to get him back. And soon."

"We might help you with that. Just... don't go anywhere." Thalasia got to her feet and went in search of Seru, gathering some fruit along the way. She found him just inside the woods.

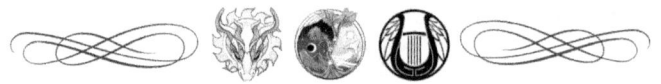

Seru ventured to the forest's edge, following the trace of radiant energy Aurelia left in her wake. He might not be an actual dragon, but he still scented and tasted that golden energy, warm and sweet like honey.

He turned at the sound of someone's approach. "Back so soon?" he asked, glad to have Thalasia back. Though they'd only been apart for a few moments, he realized he yearned for her presence and experienced an empty sensation, a feeling of being incomplete whenever she left.

Eyeing her arms overflowing with fruit, he tilted his head in mock suspicion. "Are those an offering of apology for accidentally slaughtering our green-feathered companion, or did all that healing and charming cause you to work up an appetite?"

Cracking a wide grin, she snickered. Thalasia held out a piece of fruit. "Definitely the latter, but I had to remind myself he might be the last male siren. I found out something interesting though. And it absolutely answers why they kidnapped Felix. He's been around as long as the barrier has. At least I think that's what he meant."

Seru graciously accepted the fruit. He couldn't eat it, but it didn't feel right to refuse a gift. No matter how small. She'd thought of him, and that was enough. "Thank you. That confirms what we already suspected. They're after his knowledge."

"You're welcome." She took one piece of fruit and bit into it.

He worried how far the dark guilers would go to obtain that information. The old man likely had some measure of resilience and strength. Otherwise, he wouldn't have survived the War and lived this long. Still, leaving him to be maimed and tortured by those darker elementals didn't seem right. They needed to locate Aurelia and get to rescuing him as soon as possible.

"Aurelia definitely went in search of the fae," he informed Thalasia, gesturing at the trail before foolishly realizing she likely couldn't sense the energy.

"Maybe with our combined eyes, we can get a better sense of which way she traveled. It's going to take all of us to get him back. We all seem to be on the same page about where they took him." She shifted her eyes to him. "If Aurelia can heal any wounds inflicted on him, then maybe we could go one way and they go another?"

Seru led the way, following the glitter trail. "I can track her movements. It shouldn't be too challenging to locate her." He stepped through the tall grass, holding a branch for Thalasia. "She can heal, but we have to persuade her to help another. That will be the hard part. Guilers are earthbound. Dragons see them as unworthy. Lower than servants and even prisoners. Convincing her that helping the guilers and Mac, who's itching to pick a fight with us, is going to be challenging."

She continued eating as they weaved their way through the thickening trees, stepped over ferns, and dodged bushes. "Maybe we just have to be honest with her about what we've discovered. That he could be the key to defeating them... permanently."

He kept an out for branches as they walked. "Also, you may wish to find a better hiding place for your charm. If it's metal, it can't be good for you to keep it embedded in your flesh for so long."

"It's gold. And it may not be, but I can't take a risk in it being found, especially if it is some sort of key. I still have to find the pieces to repair it."

"Aurelia might help you there. Gold is one of many items worthy of a dragon hoard," Seru said. "If one noble possesses strings to repair your lyre, she'll know and may even be the only one to have the authority to request they part with such a treasure."

"As long as she doesn't try to take it." She kept her wings tight against her back and glanced at Seru.

He crossed into a clearing with Thalasia right behind him. The radiant energy coalesced around a lone figure at its far side. Aurelia appeared to be speaking. Talking to herself? Or was there someone else there?

"Dragons store parts of themselves in whatever objects they hoard. The items become extensions of them, so stealing from them is extremely unwise. They can sense their parts and will hunt them down in the unlikely event a thief can successfully steal the object. A few in centuries past made a game of baiting other species into stealing from their hoard just to satisfy their murderous desires."

Thalasia sized up the young woman across the way. "I wouldn't want to steal anything that didn't belong to me. I've done it in the past, but only out of necessity. Nature provides a lot, just not clothes."

Seru's lips quirked into a half smile. "You are from a much more modest society than us." He called out to Aurelia, but she'd already noticed them and headed their way.

"Not by choice," Thalasia mumbled under her breath, dropping her gaze to the last two pieces of fruit.

Seru offered the piece of fruit he still carried. "I appreciate your gift, but I believe it'll do you more good than it'll do me." He gave her a smile before bowing to greet Aurelia.

Thalasia blushed as she took it back. "Thank you."

"I hope you've discovered more than the buffet." Aurelia growled, her hands on her hips. She glanced back to the trees, distracted by whatever lie beyond.

"We've discovered a great deal," he gritted his teeth as he rose. "The *buffet* was on the way, a reward for a thorough job well done. Mostly thanks to Thalasia, her mastery of healing, and her charms."

Reaching over, Thalasia set her hand on Seru's shoulder and squeezed it. She shifted her gaze to Aurelia and took a bite of the fruit Seru had just handed her. "Do you always just assume the worst? Or that we're useless pets who can't accomplish anything on our own?"

"Yes," Aurelia said.

Seru fought not to roll his eyes. "Matriarch, I have a request."

Aurelia turned back to him. "Yeah, what is it?"

"We're in need of a few golden strings," Seru replied. "You wouldn't know a noble in possession of such a treasure, would you?"

"Golden strings?" Aurelia regarded him. "What for?"

"I'm afraid I can't share the specifics—"

"No."

He frowned at her interruption. He opened his mouth to protest, but she cut him off again.

"I don't know of a noble with such a ridiculous trinket," she feigned thoughtfulness. "However, I have heard rumors of golden marvels belonging to a certain Sun God." She finished with a sly smile.

Seru cringed at the mention.

Thalasia cracked a smile for the briefest of moments before it faltered. She sighed heavily before moving to another topic. "We've figured out Felix was kidnapped and taken back to Candescent Isle. He seems to be the key to defeating the guilers, especially since we know they can get around the bridge."

Aurelia cocked her head to one side. "Let me get this straight. You want to use *my* army to invade a foreign land we know nothing about to save one measly *earthbound*?"

She sounded about as delighted as he expected at the news. "Perhaps something more... covert—"

"Out of the question."

"That *earthbound* is over three-hundred-years-old. He's got to have the answers we need to get the barrier back up. And between the four of us, we split up and cover more ground." Thalasia had put the thought out there. All they could do was wait and see.

"He's not the only one," Aurelia informed her. "Surely, there are others,"—She regarded Seru as she spoke "who are less trouble to retrieve—"

"Yes," Seru interjected, embarrassed or insecure about something. "But not another guiler. Each species has its own secrets. Surely you know this."

Aurelia narrowed her eyes at him. "Intimately."

That one word clearly made Seru uncomfortable. It struck him an invisible blow, not unlike the reaction elicited by the collar. Aurelia's accusation was clearly directed at him.

Thalasia grasped Seru's hand and gave it a squeeze. "*We* need to help Mac rescue Felix. The guiler we spoke with... he made it clear that they won't stop coming here. There's more going on than we know with the other species. They're all linked to the bridge and the barrier. Whether you like it, *we* need to work with the earthbound, unless the safety of your people matters that little to you. And just think of all the unknown places you'll get to see."

"Great. Then let *them* take on some of the responsibility and risk. So far, you, Seru, and I have been doing all the work, putting ourselves and *my* people at risk. If this is truly a battle involving all species like you claim, where are the supplies, troops, and aid should we require it? I don't see that green chicken strutting over here cooperating or offering to do much of anything other than delay our progress, so you might heal his people. So far, they've only used your abilities and Seru's to their benefit. You interrogate their prisoner and get the information needed, and you've *both* likely over shared in the time we've been apart—we're not a charity."

Seru bowed his head. "I've shared nothing that would violate my oath to you or the Cloud Court. Thalasia isn't of our lands, so she's working under whatever means necessary to resolve these issues as they arise through collaborating with not just her species, but all we've encountered. We'd still be sitting on the beach if not for her willingness to set aside her own feelings and pride."

"The barrier might still be intact if not for her, in case you've forgotten!" Aurelia argued. "Don't think just because you've grown fond of her that she's not still keeping things from you—from us—as she has from the start. She's a grifter, not a saint. So, you keep kissing her feet and singing her praises until her deceptions get you ousted or killed."

Thalasia's grip on Seru's hand tightened. She glowered at Aurelia. "Stop calling us fucking chickens. I'm not going around calling you a damn lizard," she spat out. "I'm sick and tired of every word that comes out of your mouth, beginning and ending with an insult. You don't know any more than I do that I'm to blame for the barrier. And everyone on the isle is impacted. Not just you and your people. As for Seru, I would do nothing intentionally to put his life in harm's way. Yes, I may drift, but that's because I've had to in order to protect myself and survive. I don't have people at my beck and call to wait on me hand and fucking foot. I have me, which is all I've had for years. That doesn't mean it's how I want it to be. But the gods and goddesses didn't give me that luxury. They put me in a cage of their making and expected me to be dutiful, no matter the risk. And—"

"Good stones, you three are long-winded," Mac interjected from a tree branch just behind them. He hopped down and landed on the ground with ease.

He walked over to where Thalasia stood and grabbed the last piece of fruit from her hands without touching her. "Let me clear a few things up. Dark guilers need their element close by for their magic to work. The ones here, not all of them do. They can create their element out of nothing. Felix knows how to get them there. He also knows how to take the barrier down permanently."

Mac bit into the fruit. "It's been prophesied to come down for centuries. Almost as long as her arrival has been foretold." He gestured to Thalasia and then glanced between the two women. "I only need one of you to go with me to Candescent Isle and retrieve Felix. I don't care... no, that's not true." His gaze flicked to Aurelia with a smug grin. "I prefer you. I really don't want to be around *her* when her pheromones start."

"Come again?" Aurelia asked, crossing her arms. "Prophecy? Pheromones? What are you rambling about?"

Seru gave Thalasia a one-armed hug by draping their entwined limbs over her head to rest around her shoulders as she leaned into him ever so slightly. He sympathized with her lack of patience with the two and the endless demands. But he was equally eager to hear more of Mac's tale. They just had to hang in there a little longer, and hopefully they'd come to an agreeable resolution.

"Like no other, one so pure; With a touch of gold; That holds the cure; Will one day return to the fold." Mac recited the prophecy as if he'd been forced to endure hours of memorization techniques. "Sirens were the ones who erected the barrier. Only a siren could've opened it. There are two parts—the book and the key. The book was buried somewhere here on the isle, while they took the key off. Felix knows how to find the book. It contains all the prophecies and instructions on destroying the barrier." He bit into the fruit again and looked between the three of their expectant faces. "Oh? Right. Pheromones. She's of mating age. Female sirens go through their first reproductive cycle within the first five years of adulthood. No male can help but respond once it starts."

Thalasia's cheeks flushed at the information.

"And there you have it. Barrier coming down, all *her* fault!" Aurelia gestured to Thalasia, triggering Seru to tighten his grip on her.

A low growl reverberated from deep within his belly. He forcibly settled his raised hackles but didn't conceal his fangs. "That doesn't make this all her fault, Aurelia. Nor is it only her problem. It's *our* problem. All of us. Sirens, dragons, fae, manticores—all of us."

"Key. Catalyst. Whatever you want to call it. Hand it over." Aurelia stuck out her hand at Thalasia expectantly.

Seru positioned himself between them. "Thalasia will keep the key."

"You know where it is." Aurelia glared at him. It wasn't a question, but an accusation.

"In turn," Seru said mostly to Mac, "when the book is found, it belongs to me. That way, no one of us is holding all the pieces. Once Felix is found, we agree he returns with you."

"He just stated that the *sirens* are the problem, so why would we trust them with *any* of the pieces?"

Mac pinched the bridge of his nose and groaned. "You three realize we're in the fae forest and they watch everything that happens here. Good stones, I can't believe I'm dealing with this." He focused on Aurelia. "They separated the pieces for a reason. To avoid having one species with all the power. No one species is better than the other. So, decide. You or her. I don't care which, but we're wasting time arguing over who gets what. And right now, as much as it pains me to say this, I agree with the boyfriend." He gestured to Seru.

Thalasia frowned and glanced at Mac from her position behind Seru. "You're wasting your breath on Aurelia. As far as she's concerned, everyone is beneath her. She's perfect and everyone else is the problem. I'm understanding why we have so many wars."

"You should travel with Mac," Seru interceded before Aurelia responded by setting the forest on fire. "You're more in control of your powers than I am of mine, and you'll likely need them to infiltrate Candescent Isle. Thalasia and I can handle things here. We still have a village worth of guilers to heal and will work on gathering allies from the remaining species."

Stepping from behind Seru, Thalasia nodded her agreement. "There's a lot of work to be done on both ends."

Mac crossed his arms. "Sounds like a plan to me. Come on, blondie. Let's go."

Aurelia stayed put a moment before reaching into the folds of her dress. She retrieved the crystal remnants of the fallen star, which she'd confiscated from Enoch. She placed it into Seru's palm. "There should be enough magic in that crystal to hold you steady and amplify your precious bluebird's healing so she doesn't deplete her energy. You'd better know what you're doing," Aurelia whispered harshly before begrudgingly falling in with the green siren.

Seru accepted the sparkling stone, and it glowed softly in his palm. "Thank you."

Thalasia opened her mouth to speak, but Mac waved her off dismissively. "I got it. Stay above the clouds. Watch for flying objects. Later, Thal." He winked at her and turned to Aurelia. "Shall we?"

Mac shot off to the sky, flying upwards as he blended into the forest greenery. He dodged branches and leaves until he reached the heavens.

Glaring as he took off, Thalasia smirked. "I really don't like that guy."

Aurelia raced after the green siren, sparing a last worried glance at Seru before going on her way.

Seru waited until they were out of sight before turning to Thalasia. He tucked the crystal safely into his shirt with a grin. "I think our plan to ditch Pain One and Pain Two was a success."

Thalasia leaped into his arms, embracing him tightly as she hugged her wings around him. "Yes, it was."

He laughed in response to her excitement, wrapping his arms around her. He was glad they'd stayed together and hoped Aurelia and Mac burned off their excess energy while completing their mission.

They meant well, but their execution left a lot to be desired.

To Be Continued...

In Book Four
Siren's Curse

Siren's Curse

"I don't mean to embarrass you further," Seru said, his voice faltering. "But if there's ever anything I can do to help with your siren pheromones, or anything else." He smiled clumsily. "Please, don't hesitate to ask."

Her temperature spiked rapidly as a searing flash of heat coursed through her. Her cheeks flushed. She pulled back slightly, her eyes meeting his. "I ... um..." Thalasia's gaze dropped for a moment. While she knew what was happening with her body, she couldn't very well tell him that. Not without explaining everything. Considering she'd learned about sex at the ripe age of ten, she didn't want to dredge that up. The conversation had been short and somewhat disturbing at that age. "You might notice them before me. I don't know what will happen exactly." She bit her bottom lip. "Seru, I'm untouched."

He tilted his head, with a questioning expression on his face. He buried his face in the curve of her neck and retrieved a pleasant whiff of her sweet sandalwood scent. Nestling into her, he trailed his fangs along her skin before he placed a light kiss on her neck.

Her lids lowered. His hot breath sent a shudder through her body. Thalasia licked her lips and raked a hand through his mane.

He raised his eyes and looked back at her, his gaze locking with hers. "You smell and taste just fine to me."

She brushed a soft kiss across the skin closest to his ear and whispered, "That goes both ways."

A contented rumble left his mouth. Touching nose to nose with her, he couldn't stop smiling. He stared into her eyes longer. "Guess we should tend to the severely wounded before getting some rest? We can deal with minor injuries in the morning."

A nod followed her smile, wider and brighter than it had been since their first encounter. Not that she could say for sure, but she thought her eyes might have glowed just a touch. Warmth radiated from behind her irises. "We can decide on our next move then, too."

He dipped his chin in approval, but didn't budge, taking both her hands in his.

Thalasia canted her head, her gaze fixed on his captivating blue eyes and the emotions swirling within them. She thought back to Aurelia's comment about her drifting. Her visions had always been a part of her, and she couldn't change that. What did that mean for them? "What are you thinking about?"

"Ah…" He blinked a few times. "I was just thinking." Seru paused. "About us."

"Me, too." She chewed on the inside of her cheek, debating how much to tell him. No part of their road would be easy. But she couldn't hide everything forever. Then she remembered something her father once told her after their many moves. The corners of her lips lifted into a small, almost imperceptible smile. "We have a lot of obstacles ahead. That's for sure. And I don't know that I'll ever have one place to call home, but that doesn't mean *we* can't have one. When I was little, my father told me, 'Home isn't a place you lay your head; it's a feeling you have with someone.'"

His eyes lit up. "Hmm, I like your father already." Seru kissed her forehead.

"He was a good man." Both of her parents had been good people, strong and faithful. Even in the short time she'd had with them, they had taught her a lot.

"You must miss them terribly," Seru said, drawing her into a tight embrace. He rested his chin on top of her head.

With her hands clasped around his waist, she could feel the steady thrum of his heart. "It's easier when I don't think about them. I can't always stop the memories, but I never want to forget them."

"Do you see them? In your visions, I mean?"

"No. I don't see the past, only the future where I'm meant to go." Funny. Of all the things she'd seen over the years, the night of their murders—it was the one vision she'd never received.

"I'm sorry," he murmured into her hair.

Thalasia wiped at the unshed tears, her shoulders slumping slightly. She inhaled and exhaled a deep breath. "I can't change the past, but I can choose to focus on the present and the future."

Seru squeezed his eyes shut. The lines in his forehead creased and his skin rippled.

Oh, this wasn't good. It couldn't be, yet it seemed like his beast was trying to escape. She never wanted to do this without his permission, but she had to gain control of the situation quickly. Thalasia cupped his face, the feel of his skin soft beneath her fingers, and started singing a love song from her childhood. It didn't respond well to her charm. His eyes snapped open. An electrifying pair of blazing white orbs met her gaze as a ferocious snarl escaped Seru's mouth.

She stopped singing. That didn't work the way she'd hoped, leaving her with one other option. Thalasia clenched his arms, her thumbs gently caressing his skin as she stared into his eyes. "I know you want out. And you're beautiful when you're free. I want you free, too. But right now, I need him here with me. I need you to work with us. I can't help him if you take over. Please, please let him come back."

The beast growled low, its tongue flicking between its teeth. Scales in varying shades of white and gray traveled up his arms where she touched. Seru tilted his head.

At least it looked like her male. If she didn't count the change in his eye color, his altered skin, or even the way he eyeballed her. Almost as if it couldn't decide whether she would make a tasty snack or if it wanted to nuzzle her with affection. As she preferred the latter, she continued stroking his arms where the scales appeared. "I enjoyed our time in the sky earlier. It's something I'd like to do again soon. Right now, I need Seru back. He needs you to share with him. Can you do that? Can you let him come back for now? And we'll go flying again soon."

The beast snapped at the air, irritated. It lifted its nose, inspecting her scent. Somehow, her words had broken through. Whether it was the promise of flight or something else, she couldn't say for sure. The reptilian eyes, once rimmed with yellow, faded back to Seru's standard blue, though they remained unfocused. As the beast recoiled, Seru's body went limp in her arms, his muscles refusing to hold him up without the beast's assistance.

Thalasia held him as much as her strength allowed. She slowly lowered them both to the ground and stroked his head. They could just sit here for a minute while she figured out how to get him settled somewhere—without giving all of her power away or the truth of her family line.

The gemstone Aurelia had given Seru glowed through his clothing. Seru's breaths came slowly and raggedly. "Sorry," he apologized, still unable to regain full control of his body.

"It's okay. We can sit here for a bit. I'm just glad you're back." She brushed a soft kiss across his forehead, feeling the warmth of his skin, and continued to stroke his head. There must have been some kind of internal struggle she hadn't seen Seru go through with his beast. She also didn't know what brought the beast forward to begin with, but they could address that later. Right now, it was more important he regain enough strength for them to get back to the village. The other option, she carried him to the top of the closest tree to rest.

"I... once I can stand," he amended. "I need to go away. For just a little while." Seru still had trouble catching his breath. However, his extremities moved a little.

"Oh, okay." Right. He needed to regroup. Even though she didn't like the idea of being apart, she could understand it. She eyed the collar. They hadn't thought this all the way through, had they? Aurelia knew how to deal with it. She didn't. One obstacle she'd spoken of earlier.

It took effort, but he sat up. "I've neglected feeding—eating," Seru corrected, "for far too long."

With a nod, Thalasia brought her braid over her shoulders, her fingers finding comfort in the rough texture of her hair's ends. "I noticed you didn't eat the fruit. I take it that's not part of your diet."

He offered her a bittersweet smile. "Not exactly." Reaching over, he calmed her fidgeting hands. "Saint beasts thrive on battlefields, not in everyday life." He frowned, unable to look her in the eye. "While dragons—like Aurelia—survive on a diet of fish and occasional fruits and vegetables, I can't."

She cupped his jaw and lifted his gaze to hers. "Please don't hide. Not from me. I knew you were different, but it's part of what makes you, well, you. If we gain our strength a little differently, then that's okay."

"That's easy to say when your dinner doesn't die screaming." He grimaced, giving her hand a light squeeze.

That wasn't what she had expected. It didn't bother her as much as it bothered him. Scooting a little closer to him, she opened her mouth and snapped it shut. She glanced over her shoulder toward the village, realizing nature provided in unique ways, and then she faced him. "How much sustenance do you think a dark guiler would provide?"

He glanced at her out of the corner of his eye. "Not much," he said. "Maybe if there were a thousand of them." He paused for a moment before offering a small smile. "Besides, I think that one is more likely to give me indigestion and heartburn rather than sustenance. Mac would never let me live it down if I ate him. Not to mention, the villagers would recognize me for what I am. And that could pose more trouble than the invasion from Candescent Isle."

She chuckled. "Maybe if you didn't have a siren at your side, one who's fantastic at manipulation, if I say so myself."

He bumped shoulders with her. "You're magnificent. But wiping away the most basic instinct of true unbridled fear in anyone—much less an entire village—is a very tall order. You'd be altering who they are, and I'd never ask you to bear that burden."

"Not quite what I had in mind. Manipulate the guard's memory and keep the others asleep." She nudged him. "Just a thought, you know." She beamed, quite proud of her idea, since it was still nighttime.

"I appreciate it," Seru said. "But I don't think there's even a viable source nearby. These people have lost so much already. They couldn't spare the livestock. And attacking another species is out of the question."

She laid her head on his shoulder. It left little in the way of options. "You could hunt here in the forest, but I keep thinking about what Mac said... fae."

Seru nodded.

"How much of the forest belongs to them?" She was unfamiliar with the terrain, not entirely at least, and the map couldn't help her with that, although she didn't believe it covered the entire island.

He reached out, panning his palm across the treeline. "They reside primarily in the western and southern sectors of the isle. They're a secluded species—not unlike the dragons and sirens. Tricky little bastards," he muttered. "Always watching, always listening."

Her shoulders slumped a little. They had been in the forest a good hour or longer. And shared a lot. "So then, if you head east, you should find something."

"More shape shifters and chimeras," Seru said, continuing to mark the land with his hand. "To the northeast are the manticores. Just north, the half-breeds and farther north in the sky are the true sirens—like you." He smiled. "There is an abundance of lesser species, but most of them cohabitate with the major species."

Yeah, a true siren, like me. If only he knew. His mention of the half-breeds reminded her of the war that had occurred between them and the *true* sirens, forcing them apart. Snickering at her thoughts, she laced their fingers together. "But there should be stock for hunting. You just have to keep from being seen."

"I'm as large as a mountain in my beast form. You'd have to be blind, deaf, and really dumb—" He shook his head. "I'll likely go out to sea. It's a risk, especially with the dark guilers in play, but it's safer than going inland and disappearing."

She raised an eyebrow at him. As if she could forget all about his size. "I think you're perfectly stunning." Fishing. Although in his case, maybe the bigger mammals would be better. It had been a while since she'd been along the ocean, dragging her feet and fingers through the water.

Seru's eyes widened, his expression one of shock and surprise. He spun away.

Lifting her head, she studied him for a moment. He had once told her he was like a spectator. His reaction said otherwise. She caressed his cheek, her fingertips tracing the contours of his skin. "Did you hear what I said to your beast?"

He leaned into her touch. "I did, but I couldn't act on it," he whispered. "The beast has a mind and will of its own."

"I kind of figured. It's why I just tried to talk to him and get him to work with us. Being up there with both of you, I think it helped. We may have a mission here, but that doesn't mean we can't take time for *us*, including him." It might be the only answer they had at the moment. Eventually, she'd get the collar off, and they needed to prepare for the aftermath before they got there.

"It doesn't scare you?" His words were barely audible as he pressed her hand to his lips.

"No. Not at all. No part of you scares me." She straddled him and rested her hands on his shoulders, wanting to ensure he understood exactly what she was about to tell him. "I could bury my fingers in your mane, run my hands over your smooth scales, and even wrap my arms around your powerful neck as wide as they'd go. You're gorgeous, no matter which form you're in."

"What... are you?" Seru asked her in disbelief. His hands found her hips, pulling her closer.

Oh, that was such a loaded question. She beamed at him, and a shiver trickled down her spine. Her fingers dug into his shoulders ever so slightly as the feathers on her wings ruffled. "I'm just me."

"In all my years, I've encountered nothing like you," he said, kissing her forehead once more.

She wrapped her arms around his neck and ran her fingers through his dark hair. For the first time, she felt like there could be more to her life, that maybe what her parents had, she could have, too. "It goes both ways."

Seru pulled back, clearing his throat, a visible shudder running through him. "I really should hunt down dinner before my beast decides you look like a very different meal."

"And I should check on the villagers. See if there are any that need healing." She sighed. "Then I'm going to find a tree big enough for two."

Seru smiled as he reached into his pocket to retrieve the crystal. "Here, take this with you." He pressed it into her palm, closing her fingers around it and bringing her fist to his lips. "I'll find you when I return."

Tucking the crystal into her pants pocket, she dipped her chin. While she had one other place to put it, she couldn't do it without drawing attention to her purse. "You better." Thalasia grinned as she climbed out of his lap and held out a hand to help him up.

He took her hand, though she suspected it wasn't really necessary. Seru rose to his feet, stretching his weary limbs, then enveloped her in one last, lingering embrace.

Demeter. She didn't think she'd ever tire of being in his arms. Thalasia wrapped her wings around him, inhaling his familiar scent as she closed her eyes and listened to the steady thrum of his heartbeat.

"Be good," Seru told her as her wings unfurled from around him. He took a few steps back before shifting into the clouds and disappearing into the night.

"Be safe," she called after him, though she quickly brought her attention back to the present. There was work to do, so she turned and flew toward the village.

About the Authors

Author of the Love's Worth Series, **Brigit Rosé,** lives in a world of romance. She has taken her life experience and made it into one endless love story. When she's not writing, she's singing loudly and off-key, hanging out with friends, or playing with her 2 fur babies. She can usually be found with a kiss in one hand and a twist of line in the other, exactly the stories she likes to read and write. If you'd like to know more about Brigit, you can find out more on her website: https://kbfennerrose.com

Nikki Haras has had a passion for writing since she was a small child. She will use whatever means necessary to get the words down that swirl inside her head, bleeding ink onto the page and breathing life into the characters who demand to tell their stories. When she's not immersing herself in her fantasy worlds, she's a full-time mom of three children and three fur babies, but you can usually always find her with a cup of coffee in one hand and a pen tucked into her messy bun. Always plotting the next amazing scene, fantastic new story, or immersive fantasy world to bring to life. To find out more about Nikki Haras and her upcoming book releases, you can find her on Facebook.

Other Works by Brigit Rosé

Under Krys Fenner

Co-authored

Coming soon

Blood & Bondage (The Empyreal Den Chronicles)
Jail Break (The Atlis Chronicles)
Bloodline (Prisme Isle Series Prequel)
Siren's Curse (Prisma Isle Series)
Silencing the Shape Shifter (Prisma Isle Series)
Kingdom of Embers (Prisma Isle Series)
Darkness Reconciled (Prisma Isle Series)
Seized by the Heart (Prisma Isle Series)

www.ingramcontent.com/pod-product-compliance
Lightning Source LLC
Chambersburg PA
CBHW071131100726
47908CB00008B/2566